THIS IS MIDNIGHT

BERNARD TAYLOR was born in Swindon, Wiltshire, and now lives in London. Following active service in Egypt in the Royal Air Force, he studied Fine Arts in Swindon, then at Chelsea School of Art and Birmingham University. On graduation he worked as a teacher, painter and book illustrator before going as a teacher to the United States. While there, he took up acting and writing and continued with both after his return to England. He has published ten novels under his own name, including *The Godsend* (1976), which was adapted for a major film, and *Sweetheart, Sweetheart* (1977), which Charles L. Grant has hailed as one of the finest ghost stories ever written. He has also written novels under the pseudonym Jess Foley, as well as several works of nonfiction. He has won awards for his true crime writing and also for his work as a playwright. *There Must Be Evil*, his latest true crime study, was recently published in England.

Taylor's classics *The Godsend*, *Sweetheart, Sweetheart*, *The Reaping*, and *The Moorstone Sickness* are available from Valancourt, as is his newest thriller, *The Comeback* (2016), the author's triumphant return to fiction after a long hiatus.

I0609707

* Available from Valancourt Books

THIS IS MIDNIGHT

stories by

BERNARD TAYLOR

VALANCOURT BOOKS

This Is Midnight by Bernard Taylor
Originally published in hardcover by Centipede Press in July 2017
First Valancourt Books edition 2019

Copyright © 2017 by Bernard Taylor

Published by Valancourt Books, Richmond, Virginia
http://www.valancourtbooks.com

ISBN 978-1-948405-39-3 (*trade paperback*)

Also available as an electronic book.

All Valancourt Books publications are printed on acid free paper that
meets all ANSI standards for archival quality paper.

Set in Dante MT

CONTENTS

This is Midnight
Let no star delude us
Dawn is very far. . .

Rudyard Kipling

INTRODUCTION

How pleased I am to have my handful of short stories brought together – for better or worse.

As for the writing of them, I can't speak for other writers, of course, but my own embarking on a short story was never a planned exercise. The story, or the germ of it, would usually come springing from something observed, or something heard or read about – sometimes the most trivial happening, at other times something a little more momentous.

The few short tales that I have written, and which are here in these pages, mostly came from the period before I turned my attention to writing full-length works. And, as it so happened, in several cases a particular short story would lead in time to a full length novel.

On my return from the USA in the late sixties I was for the most part working as an actor, while during those periods when I was 'resting' – as out-of-work actors have it – I was glad to spend the odd day, week or month as a supply/substitute teacher, at schools in the East End of London.

It was about this time that I became friends with a professional writer who had published several novels as well as a number of short stories – horror stories, all of them. And why don't you, he said to me one day, try writing a horror story? Well, I said, I would if I had an idea for one.

And then it happened. A few days later, in the classroom at the school where I was currently spending a few days as a teacher, one of my pupils, sitting at her desk, gave a wide yawn. And I could see at once that she was also chewing. But it was not this prohibited act that got my sharp attention; it was the appearance of the gum in her open mouth. A pale, greenish colour, for a brief moment I could see it stretched across the inside of her gaping mouth like some unbelievably grotesque living creature.

And so I went home that night and wrote a story, to be published later as 'Our Last Nanny.'

I mention this little incident simply as an example of how the most fleeting, banal and trivial occurrence can sometimes lead to the germ of an idea – in this particular case leading to the first of my stories to be published.

But the second of my tales sprang from something altogether much deeper, darker – an incident that stayed with me, and remains with me today. And perhaps it will be of interest to my readers now to have this extra little short story to add to those that are to come.

Paula Hawkins' novel *The Girl on the Train*, is of course, and deservedly so, a best-seller – concerning a young woman who observes an interesting ongoing situation from her train window on her daily commute. And something with a similar shadowy tone once happened to me. But while my tale would not include the observance of any crime, crime was certainly embedded in my view, and in my case the ghost of real, actual crime.

It happened one dark night in the late nineteen-sixties as I made my way home through the streets of the Ladbroke Grove area of west London. It had been raining all evening, but now the rain had stopped. There was no sign of a moon, and in the dank, gloomy streets the pale yellow lamplight reflected dully in the wet pavements. To my irritation, I found I was lost. I had been visiting friends for dinner nearby and now, trying to make my way by means of a short cut to the Tube station, I had somehow taken a wrong turning, with the result that there came the sudden realisation that I didn't know where I was.

I was not at all familiar with the area; all about me was strange. I walked on, searching for some landmark or other familiar sight, heading in what I thought must be somewhere in the right direction. And then, turning a corner, I found myself at the entrance to a dark little cul-de-sac. In the gloom, I could just make out the name of the place, and saw that I was standing at the entrance to Ruston Close.

At once in my head the name rang some tenebrous little bell. And in a second it came to me that this half-hidden, little dead-end street had not so long before boasted the home of John Reginald Christie, one of England's most notorious serial killers, hanged in 1953 for his crimes. The original name of the cul-de-sac was in fact Rillington Place, with Christie and his sad, doomed wife living at number 10. *10 Rillington Place*. Just the sound of those words brought its own frisson, as it does still today.

Not surprisingly, following Christie's execution the name of the street had been changed in an attempt to dissociate it from the catalogue of dreadful horrors that had taken place there, horrors with which it would for ever be associated.

Much has since been written about Christie's evil doings, and by coincidence, even as I write these words the BBC is preparing to broadcast yet another dramatization of the events that took place under the bloody hands of this most infamous man.

Anyway, there I was, some fifty or so years ago, standing in the wet darkness, lit only by a pale streetlamp, at the entrance to one of London's most notorious scenes of criminality.

And then I suddenly realised that the whole of the little street was dead, quite dead. Not only was there no sign of any living soul about, but there were no lights burning in any of the windows. I stood there. I couldn't turn about and go on my way, I couldn't pass it by, and after a minute I ventured in. My footfalls hollow on the wet cement I walked up the little dead-end street (and was there ever a more apt description of this particular cul-de-sac?), walking between the two rows of Victorian terrace houses to the one at the very end, number 10, Christie's erstwhile home, the house where the murders had been committed. And on reaching it I saw that it was in the process of being demolished. But of course. This, I realised, accounted for the dead, lifeless windows, the dark solitude of the place. For it was not only number 10 that was to go. That was merely to be the first. The whole two rows of houses, I realised, were about to be destroyed. The powers that be had clearly come to the realisation that a new name would never be enough to dispatch the horror from the spot, could never ever make this humble little street habitable again.

With Christie's house the last one in the row, I saw that its external left side abutted a high wall that stretched right across the street, and as I stood there I heard, dispelling the quiet, the sound of an approaching Tube train. Moments later it was rattling past on the other side of the barrier wall.

I stayed after the sound of the train had faded in the distance, standing looking up at the disfigured face of number 10. The demolition, I saw, was well under way. Some of the upper front wall had already been torn down, and in the gloom I could just make out the dingy interiors of the upper rooms.

After standing there staring at the wretched scene for a few moments longer, I turned and found my way back to the station, and then home.

The next morning I was called on to teach, and on my way to the school where I was to spend the next few days, I found – of all the coincidences – that my train would run on the track that lay on the other side of the wall that abutted Ruston Close and the wretched remains of number 10. And minutes later, and now in the bright sunlight, as the train rumbled past, I could see again, so close, the ruined house, with its broken walls, and I could see clearly too the flower-patterned wallpaper on the walls, wallpaper that Christie himself had no doubt hung – he being a handy man-about-the-house – and which would have helped to hide for years his dark secrets.

The frisson of my encounter with that house of death stayed with me, and on my little portable typewriter that evening I began to tap out, two-fingered, my story 'Forget-me-not.'

So much for one rather dark 'inspiration'.

Over the next two or three years I wrote most of the other tales here in this collection. Then at the suggestion of my literary agent I gathered them together and he sent them off to the publisher Souvenir Press where they were read by the company's director, the dynamic Ernest Hecht. At his encouraging suggestion I took a newly-completed story – one not yet submitted for publication – and developed it into a full-length novel. And so was published my first book, *The Godsend*.

And other stories led in time to more novels. 'Travelling Light' led to my book *The Moorstone Sickness*, while a one-act play I wrote for television (but sadly was never produced) gave me the idea for *One of the Family*, and from there to my novel *Sweetheart, Sweetheart*.

One of the last of my stories, 'Mama's Boy,' came from an incident when, in my work as an actor, and on location in Italy, I watched through my shuttered hotel window a little domestic drama unfold.

And so here they are, together at last, my short stories – and, I have to say, not offering much in the way of creeping ghouls or witches on broomsticks; not much in the way of foul wizardry or the supernatural. I think I would have to leave the production of such truly terror-inducing tales to masters such as the great M.R. James, who, I have to confess, shameless as I am, provided me with the theme of one of my novels. But that's another story.

Bernard Taylor
London, November 2016

'Out of Sorts' originally published in *The Dodd, Mead Gallery of Horror*, edited by Charles L. Grant (Dodd, Mead, August 1983).

'Mama's Boy' is original to this collection.

'Forget-Me-Not' originally published in *The Year's Best Horror Stories: Series III* edited by Richard Davis (DAW Books, July 1975).

'Our Last Nanny' originally published in *The 8th Fontana Book of Great Horror Stories*, edited by Mary Danby (Fontana, September 1973).

'Cera' originally published in *Frighteners*, edited by Mary Danby (Fontana, 1974).

'One of the Family' originally published in *The Screaming Book of Horror* (Screaming Dreams, October 2012).

'Pat-a-Cake, Pat-a-Cake' originally published in *Frighteners 2*, edited by Mary Danby (Fontana, 1976).

'My Very Good Friend' originally published in *Frighteners*, edited by Mary Danby (Fontana, 1974).

'Samhain' originally published in *Final Shadows*, edited by Charles L. Grant (Doubleday, September 1991).

'Peace Offering' is original to this collection.

'Travelling Light' originally published in *65 Great Tales of the Supernatural*, edited by Mary Danby (Octopus Books, 1979).

'Mommy's Programme' is original to this collection.

'Green Fingers' originally published March 18, 1975 as 'In the Garden of Evil' in the *London Evening News*.

OUT OF SORTS

'O H, *not the twenty-first!*' Paul Gunn said. 'Whatever made you choose *that* date?'

'I didn't *choose* it. That's the day the meeting falls – third Friday in the month.' Sylvia shook her head. 'I told you – there was nothing I could do about it.'

'You could have arranged to hold the bloody thing somewhere else, couldn't you? Does it have to be here?'

'It's *my turn*,' Sylvia said with a sigh. 'Besides, I'm president. And apart from that I just wasn't thinking, I suppose. I can't be expected to remember everything.'

'No, but I do expect you to remember the *important* things.' He made a sound of exasperation. 'Can't you change it? It's bad enough at the best of times, but when the bloody house is filled with people – '

'It's only three days away,' Sylvia said reasonably. 'Look, Paul, we planned it weeks ago and it's too late to alter it now.' She looked at him entreatingly. 'Oh, please don't be angry. You'll be all right. No one will bother you.'

He refused to be entreated or pacified, though, and she watched as he angrily snatched up his newspaper, opened it unnecessarily roughly and submerged himself in its contents. End of conversation, as always.

His large, tanned hands looked very dark against the white of the paper. It was the hair on them. Thick and black, it made his hands look larger than they were. It was probably a turn-on for some women, she thought. Not to herself, though; not now – if it had ever been . . . It was to Norma Russell, though, she was quite certain. Norma, with her model's 35 x 25 x 36 figure, her high cheek bones and sleek blonde hair. Paul's hirsute body would be just the thing to appeal to *her.*

If it came to looks, she reflected, it was quite obvious that she herself couldn't compete with anyone like Norma. Oh, once she'd been pretty in a vague, mousey kind of way, but not for years now. Well, she hadn't made any effort, had she? And why should she try, now, when there was no point?

And there was no point anymore. More than that, in her eyes it would have seemed the height of stupidity to go to the bother of dressing up, when practically the only man who ever looked at you was your husband – and even when he *did* he didn't even see you. Yes, pointless, to say the least.

Paul, on the other hand, seemed to have grown sleeker and better-looking in an overfed kind of way over the years. Success showed clearly on him; in his clothes and his body – and his women. Yes, he did look better. That, she supposed, was what contentment and complacency did. She shot him a look of hatred as he lounged, protected by the shield of his paper. Then she turned and went upstairs.

This place, too, was a sign of his success. Set apart in this tiny Yorkshire village of Tallowford, the house was huge and rambling, exquisitely furnished; further testimony to the years of effort he'd put into his engineering company, now one of the most profitable small businesses in nearby Bradford.

In her study Sylvia sat down at her elegant desk, Louis XIV, genuine. Opening her diary she looked again at the date of the meeting. The 21st. No mistake. Then she checked over the Women's Circle committee list. There would be six of them. On the past three occasions there'd been only five of them Pamela Horley, Jill Marks, Janet True, and Mary Hanley. This time, though, there'd be six again. A replacement had been found for Lilly Sloane who had moved away – a replacement proposed by her and voted in unanimously by the others: Norma Russell.

Norma, of course, had so eagerly accepted the offered place on the committee. 'Well, if you really want me and you think I can be of help,' she'd said. But she hadn't fooled Sylvia for one minute. Sylvia knew quite well that Norma's eagerness stemmed from the fact that as every third meeting was held at the Gunns' house it could only lead to more encounters between herself and Paul...

Methodically Sylvia went through the list, telephoning the members to check that each was okay for the 21st. All except Norma. *Her* number was engaged. Not that Sylvia needed to worry; if there was one member she knew she could count on, that one was Norma.

Pushing her papers away from her she turned in her chair and looked around her. No expense had been spared in this room. The rest of the furniture was as elegant as the desk on which her elbow rested, as elegant as that in the bedroom next door – the bedroom in which she slept alone – except on those nights when Paul would come to her and use her for the release of frustrations...

That's how it had gone on. That's how it *would* go on – unless something was done to stop it. Oh, she was safe enough, she knew; secure enough in the continuing of her material comforts. As much as Paul would like to see the back of her he'd never divorce her – or even leave her. He knew which side his bread was buttered, all right. Hence the comfort in which he kept her. And that, surely, was partly the reason for his resentment of her – the fact that he knew that they were irrevocably tied – in sickness and in health, for as long as they both should live – by his dependence upon her.

And why, she sometimes asked herself, didn't *she* leave *him*? But what would she do if she did? Paul wouldn't support her, and she'd been trained for no particular occupation. For the past twenty-five years she'd known only this life – marriage to a man whose gratitude for her understanding had in no time worn threadbare.

But for all of that, she thought, she could have put up with it – had it not been for his affairs. One after the other they had punctuated the years of their married life. And for that she was resentful – not just because of his infidelity and his rejection of her, but because he gave to those *other* women what he never gave, never *had* given, to her – not after the first few months of their courtship, anyway. Those other women – they were allowed to see only the *best* side of him – the cheerfulness, the gentlemanliness, the solicitousness. She, through her near-total acceptance of the real person, the person they never saw, was doomed to live with it, warts and all.

She got up from the desk and stood there in the silent room. It couldn't go on, though. And it *wouldn't*. *No*, after the 21st it wouldn't be the same. Come the 21st there'd be some changes made. Norma Russell would be the last, she'd make sure of that. After Norma there wouldn't be any more affairs.

When she got downstairs she found Paul on the phone. He started slightly when she suddenly appeared before him, and said shakily into the receiver, voice thick with guile and not a little guilt:

'Well, Frank, I think we ought to leave it until our meeting next week . . . we can discuss it fully then . . .' And Sylvia smiled to herself as she went by him, realizing why Norma's telephone had been engaged, and at the realization that *they* thought she was so easily fooled. Not she. *Frank*, indeed. She was a lot smarter than they dreamed. Certainly a damn sight smarter than that vacuous, simpering Norma with her Gucci shoes, Charlie perfume, and Dior sunglasses. Norma Russell, with her sophisticated approach and smug, know-it-all manner didn't know it all by any means.

Not yet. She would in time.

Paul left his office early that Friday, came into the house and flopped down onto the sofa saying he had a headache. From past experience Sylvia guessed well enough how he was feeling, but any sympathy she once might have felt for him had long ago vanished.

They ate an early dinner and as soon as it was over he went upstairs to the attic. Sylvia followed after a while, and quietly opened the door and looked in. He was sound asleep. Backing out again, she turned the key and softly pushed home the heavy bolts. For a second she listened, her ear to the door, but no sound came to her through the thick, heavy oak. After a moment she turned and went back downstairs to get ready for the meeting.

The women all arrived within a few minutes of each other around eight o'clock, and with the coffee already made they got down fairly quickly to the business of the evening. That business was the forthcoming summer fête and the Women's Circle's part in it. The discussion went smoothly, and so it should have, for each of them – with the exception of Norma – had helped organize a dozen similar events in the past.

Finally, after much discussion and note-taking it seemed to be all sorted out. Sylvia summed up the results of their discussion.

'All right, then,' she said, 'I think that's it. So you, Pam, and you, Janet, will get together and organize the refreshments and the baking competition. And you, Jill and Mary, will work on the jumble. And you all know your individual tasks.' Smiling at Norma, who returned the smile, she went on: 'And that leaves Norma and me to take care of the Fancy Goods and the white elephant stall. Is that okay?'

The next forty minutes were spent in drinking more coffee and generally talking over the finer points of their various tasks. There was much talk of 'willing hands' and 'helpers' and 'generous donors'; various names were bandied about, and there were the endlessly expressed hopes that on the day the weather would be kind to them. Sylvia began to get the feeling that the meeting would never end; never before had the conversation of her friends seemed quite so meaningless. But there, never before had she herself had quite such serious matters on her mind.

At last, though, it was nine-forty-five, and the meeting was over. As they all got up to go, chattering their goodnights, Sylvia caught at Norma's sleeve, saying, 'Oh, Norma – are you in a particular hurry to get away?'

Norma's eager-to-please expression didn't fool Sylvia for

one moment. 'Not at all,' she said. 'Why? Is there something else I can do?' Now she was like the cat that had found the cream; not only had she been voted onto the committee but she had furthermore been chosen to work closely with Sylvia. From now on she'd have a cast-iron excuse for phoning or calling at the house at practically any time.

Sylvia smiled as sweetly and as naturally as she could under the circumstances. 'I was just wondering whether you'd care to stay behind for a little while so that we can go over – in more detail – a few of the things that you and I will be looking after . . .'

'Of course, I'd be glad to. Anytime at all, Sylvia. You just let me know.' She'd picked up her bag but now she set it down again at the side of the sofa.

'Fine,' said Sylvia. 'I'll just see the other girls out, then we can talk.'

When the other members had all gone out into the night Sylvia came back into the sitting room. As she sat down, Norma said to her: 'I suppose Paul hates being around when these – these hen parties are in session, doesn't he?'

Sylvia nodded. 'Oh, loathes it, my dear. Absolutely.'

'Does he – er – get back late . . . ?'

Oh, thought Sylvia, so obviously Norma had told Paul that she'd be coming to the meeting – and it was equally obvious that he'd told her he'd be out somewhere. Well, that was understandable. 'I'm sorry?' Sylvia said, ' – what did you ask me?'

'Paul – does he usually stay out late when you have your meetings here?'

'Oh, yes, usually he does. Not tonight, though.' That, Sylvia thought, should get her going. It did.

'Oh,' said Norma, ' – is there something different about tonight?' She sounded very casual.

Sylvia thought, Yes, you could say that. Then she said aloud, 'The poor love didn't go out this evening. He can't.'

'Oh – you mean he's still in the house?'

'Yes. He couldn't go out. He's just not up to it, poor man.' Sylvia eyed Norma's expression, seeing the look of concern that briefly clouded Norma's green eyes.

'Is he ill?' Norma asked.

'Well, not exactly ill,' Sylvia replied. 'He's just – well, just a little out of sorts.'

'Oh, dear, what a shame.' Norma sighed. 'Perhaps you should have phoned and cancelled the meeting. Won't he have been disturbed by all our chatter?'

Sylvia shook her head. 'Oh, no, don't worry about that. He won't have heard a thing. He's up in the attic.'

'In the attic?'

'Yes,' Sylvia's smile was indulgent. 'It's his little den, as he calls it. His little retreat. He's got a bed up there – well away from it all. It's much the best place for him at a time like this, when he's not himself. Anyway . . .' She pulled her notepad towards her as if to signify that it was time for them to get on with their work, then, suddenly, with a look of dismay, she dropped her pencil and clapped her hand to her mouth. 'Oh, my God!' she said.

'What's the matter?' Norma stared at her in surprise. Her concern looked genuine.

'I think I'm losing my mind,' Sylvia said. 'It's going, I swear it's going. My memory. Oh, dear.'

'What is it? What's up?'

'I promised faithfully that I'd drop a few little things over to Mrs Harrison this afternoon. Poor old lady – she can't get out, what with her bad leg, and she's got her daughter coming for lunch tomorrow. I did all her shopping for her this afternoon – and it's still out there in the kitchen.' She glanced at the clock. 'Just ten o'clock. I'll bet she's been expecting me all day. How dreadful.' She sat as if pondering for a moment, then said: 'I know she doesn't go to bed till quite late. I think I'll just give her a ring and then take the stuff round to her. I shan't get a chance in the morning, I know . . .'

Even as she finished speaking she was opening her address

book and looking up Mrs Harrison's number. She dialled it and Mrs Harrison answered almost immediately. She sounded so pleased to hear Sylvia's voice. No, she said, she wasn't in bed; she was watching the telly darts championship – adding with a little giggle that she quite liked big men. Sylvia, refusing to take no for an answer, then said that she was going to get straight on her bike and bring the groceries round. After all, it was only a couple of miles and no one ever came to harm in Tallowford.

The call at an end, Sylvia had put on her coat and was picking up the shopping basket before she seemed to remember that Norma was still there.

'Oh, Norma, my dear,' she said. 'After asking you to stay behind I now go rushing off like this. I do apologise. Whatever must you think of me?'

'I think you're a very kind person,' Norma simpered. 'That's what I think.'

And Sylvia, in spite of her loathing for the creature, found herself thinking, How very true.

She hitched the handle of the basket more securely over her arm. 'My bike's just round the side,' she said. 'I'm sorry to go dashing off like this, but I've got to go.' She paused. 'You don't mind letting yourself out, do you?'

'Of course not. Not at all.'

'Oh, bless you. And I wonder, would you be an angel and make sure that I've turned off the gas under the kettle and see that there are no cigarettes burning anywhere . . . Oh, and if Paul *should* by any chance call out, just tell him I'll be back in an hour or so – or maybe a little longer. Would you mind?' She moved to the door. 'You can let yourself out, can't you?'

'Yes, of course.'

'Oh, thank you so much. Goodnight, then.'

'Goodnight.'

Hardly hearing Norma's reply, Sylvia opened the front door and went to her bicycle in the garage. After carefully securing the basket, she got on and pedalled away. The night was so bright as she sped down the lonely country road that she really had hardly any need of her bicycle lamp at all.

From the window Norma watched the red glow of Sylvia's tail light till it disappeared. Then she made a lightning check of the gas taps and the ashtrays. Everything was fine.

Yes, everything was fine. Everything was perfect.

In the hall she stood quite still and looked up the stairs. Then, after a second or two, she began to climb. She didn't put on the lights; she didn't want to take the chance of being seen through a window by some passing villager.

So Paul was in the attic, Sylvia had said. Norma continued up the stairs, past the first floor and on up the next flight – narrower now and turning. At the top she came to a stop, hesitated a moment and then softly called out:

'Paul – ?'

Silence. And then she heard a sound. It came from the door a few yards to her right. Moving towards it she saw to her horror that there were two heavy bolts pulled across. Sylvia had locked him in! How could she?!

There was a key in the lock too. She turned it, releasing the lock. How could Sylvia have done such a thing? Some people! She turned her attention then to the bolts, and with an effort slid them back. It was done. Then, turning the handle, she opened the door a fraction.

From the faint glow filtering in from the landing she could see that there was no light in the room, and none coming in from the small, uncurtained window. 'Paul – ?' She whispered his name. She could hear him breathing, heavily, as if he was in a very deep sleep, or . . .

Opening the door wider, she stepped into the room and closed the heavy door behind her.

Now in deep darkness she whispered his name again. 'Paul?' There came no answer. 'Paul,' she said, a little louder now, ' – are you there? It's me – Norma. I've come to pay you a little surprise visit.'

The room was swallowed up in shadow. She could see nothing. She could hear nothing but the breathing.

'Paul – darling, is that you?' she said. She listened. The breathing – somehow it didn't sound like him. It didn't sound quite – right. 'Paul,' she said, 'Sylvia told me you weren't quite yourself tonight – so I've come to cheer you up a bit – if I can!' She laughed lightly, nervously into the dark. The sound of his breathing was growing louder, coming a little nearer. 'Paul,' she said, ' – oh, come on, darling. Don't fool about . . .'

Suddenly the moon, the full moon, was no longer obscured by the clouds. Suddenly the room was bathed in light. And she saw the bars at the window – thick, metal bars. She noticed, too, the complete absence of furniture. There was only straw on the floor. She became aware, too, of the strong, rank animal smell that permeated the air around her.

And then she saw Paul coming towards her.

In the brilliant silver light of the full moon he lunged towards her and she felt him reach out with one huge clawed paw, felt herself wrenched forward, towards the great snout, the great fangs that opened wide, dripping in anticipation. She heard the guttural sound from deep in his throat.

The sound that came from her own throat, a small, pleading cry of terror, was cut off before she'd hardly had a chance to utter it.

At Mrs Harrison's, Sylvia looked at her watch. It was almost eleven. She put down her cup, got to her feet and took up her empty basket. It had been so nice, she said, but she really must get back. There'd be a lot of cleaning up to do. Besides, Paul might start to wonder where she was. He didn't usually worry, but he could get very funny when he was out of sorts. There was just no telling.

'It's probably the full moon,' Mrs Harrison said with a little chuckle. 'Did you notice there's a full moon tonight? I swear it makes a difference to some people. You might not believe this, but I'm sure it used to affect my Ralph. He used to go right off his food. Wouldn't eat a thing. No appetite at all.'

Sylvia looked out of the window at the moon's big, white, smiling face. 'Oh,' she said with a little smile, 'I can't say it takes Paul like that. Just the opposite in fact. When he's not his usual self, like today – a bit out of sorts – he gets absolutely ravenous. Such an appetite you wouldn't believe! Like he hasn't eaten in a month.'

MAMA'S BOY

I HAD BEEN IN THE ROOM just a couple days when I became aware of the neighbours.

It was the noise that drew my attention at first. Not loud noise, or anything as irritating and intrusive as music or anything like that; really just little sounds of movement, of living, coming faintly into the room.

My room was on a corner of the hotel building, and the sounds came from behind a window in the east-facing wall. I couldn't see what was going on as the window had shutters and they were closed tight. I hadn't bothered to open them since my arrival, so I had no idea what was behind them. The window in the south wall gave me all the light I needed – all that glorious Florentine sunlight – plus a wonderful view down onto the busy little street below.

A small place it was, my hotel, my *pensione* – tucked away pretty much, but handy for the centre of the city. Not expensive either, and comfortable enough if you didn't expect a great deal.

I was a newcomer to Florence. In fact, I was a newcomer to Italy. I'd never set foot in the country before, and I didn't speak a word of the language. My wife and I had never been much for travelling, but now that I was widowed and alone and well into the third year of my retirement from the bank I'd decided to live a little dangerously and splash out a bit – not financially, I mean, but with my time. You're a long time dead, as people say, and I'd thought it was about time I did something, maybe saw something of the world outside of the small Kentish town where I'd spent most of my life.

Since my arrival at the hotel I'd spent hardly any time in my room – being intent on taking in as much of the beautiful city as my two weeks' stay there would allow. So for most of the time I was out, enjoying the wonderful Florentine spring, the warm sun, the friendly, welcoming natives, and the marvellous sights.

It was during my second day there, in the afternoon when, returning to my little room to take a break after a fairly exhausting morning of sightseeing, I first became aware of the sounds. I stepped over to the window, stood there for a minute, listening, then pulled the shutters open.

Like the other window, the frame held a fine wire mesh across it as a barrier against any flying insects that might be attracted to light in the room, but from my side I could see through it quite clearly, and it allowed me a perfect view of the scene beyond.

I had expected to find myself looking down onto the busy street below, but no, there was a family life going on there, and so close at hand. Just there on the other side of the screen it was all taking place, right before my eyes in the most cramped little space. Cramped and basic. There was nothing in the way of even the most modest comforts. How some others lived, I thought.

For a moment or two as I peered through the mesh I felt the faintest touch of guilt – in that I was very conscious of looking in on something that was private. I had to look, though – I couldn't not do it – the scene fascinated me. It was so completely new to me; I had never seen anything like it in my life.

Of course, if there'd been a light behind me in my room I couldn't have stood there observing what was going on. I would have been clearly visible, standing so near, and watching as closely as I was. But by good luck I hadn't switched on the light, so those on the other side couldn't see me. They were totally unaware of my presence.

There were two of them – and they were just babies. There was no parent, no adult in view at all, and it was a very still, immobile scene. During the few minutes while I stood there peering at them I didn't see either of the infants move in the slightest, not so much as an inch. They stayed just as they were, absolutely still, and made no sound, no sound at all. One of the youngsters looked, I thought, to be a little bit bigger than the other. He was noticeably bigger, in fact – and not only that, but he was more robust and more vital-looking in his appearance. I say *he*, though I couldn't tell what gender he or she was – either of them. Male or female, I hadn't a clue. This was no sweet little fairy tale nursery scene – there was no pink for a girl and blue for a boy here.

I remained there for a little while longer, watching, totally fascinated. And at the same time I think I was also hoping that something would happen – I was waiting for something to happen – something that would change the scene in some way – it was so very static. But nothing did. The two little ones stayed as they were, passive, silent, unmoving. Perhaps, the thought came to me that, like me, they were waiting.

After another minute or so I quietly closed the shutters on the silent little scene.

On my bed I lay back and closed my eyes. I'd had some hours at the Uffizi that morning and my feet were feeling the strain. I pulled a rug over me, closed my eyes and, like any self-respecting Italian who appreciated a siesta, drifted off into sleep.

When I awoke an hour or so later I lay for a while looking up at the ceiling while the sounds of the Florentine afternoon drifted up on the soft, balmy air. And then, added to the familiar sounds of the motor traffic and people's voices, came a faint noise from behind the closed shutters.

I pulled the rug aside, got up, moved across the room and as gently and quietly as I could, eased the shutters open.

The babies were not alone now. Their mother was there.

I don't know what I'd been expecting, but she wasn't much to look at. She was quite dull-looking in fact, but what she lacked in glamour she made up for in efficiency – no question of that. When I got this first glimpse of her she was in the middle of feeding the babies. And I couldn't help but observe that she looked completely single-minded as she went about it, obviously totally dedicated to the job. It was fascinating. Hardly daring to breathe, as they say, I watched her very brisk, efficient movements, and all the time I could see that neither she nor the two infants were in the slightest aware of my nearness.

I watched as she finished feeding the bigger of the two babies (Buster, as I came to think of him), and then she turned and moved back to the partly open door. Another second and she was bustling out of sight.

With Mama gone, I turned my attention back to the babes. There was Buster looking comfortable and well-fed – but what about the smaller one? I looked at him, cuddled up there next to his sibling. He looked such a pathetic, sad-looking little thing in comparison, and far less healthy-looking. Had he been fed too, I wondered? I hadn't seen her give him anything. But maybe she'd done that before I happened to look in.

The next morning I was up early again and off out – like the swarms of other visitors to the city, anxious not to miss a thing. Joining a bunch of other tourists, it was another morning of sightseeing, with a visit to a church, and another of the museums. When in Rome, as they say – or in this case Florence – you have to go with the flow. And all very interesting. Lots more paintings, statues and beautiful architecture. A fascinating experience – though of course, you wouldn't want to do it more than once. I had a bit of late lunch afterwards at a little *trattoria* and didn't get back to the hotel until almost three. I picked up my key from the desk, rode the antique, rickety little lift up to my room and let myself in. Then I walked directly to the east window and quietly, quietly eased open the shutters.

And by chance I seemed to have chosen my moment well.

Even as I bent to peer through the screen I saw the mother arrive. There was a sound from the doorway, a little scrabbling, bustling noise, and suddenly she was there; there was Mama, coming in with lunch.

Just like before, she was so efficient, the way she got on with her job. As with the first time I'd observed her there was nothing in the way of any subtle social touches; she was just there, coming in and moving straight for the two infants, the twins. No hesitation at all; it was like: *Okay, boys, here comes Mama. Get ready to eat!*

And both boys looked to be ready for it, all right. Buster in particular. The second their mother appeared he was turning to her, open-mouthed and hungry. She went straight to him, without a moment of hesitation, and began to feed him. She didn't waste any time about it, either – just got on with the job. And there was no finesse in her actions, no warmth or tenderness at all – not that I could see. She just fed him, carefully but rather coldly.

Silently I watched from my side of the screen, anxious not to do anything that might cause any alarm. What would she do if she became aware of me, I wondered? Would she have been that much bothered? The way she behaved, it was as if her whole concentration was on the business of the feeding. Oh, Mama, I thought, you are one dedicated mother, you really are.

When she had finished feeding Buster, I expected her to tend to her other babe – Tiny as I called him – and give him his feed too. He was there, eyes fixed on her, clearly waiting and wanting to be fed, but to my surprise she took no notice of him. Having finished feeding Buster, she just turned and moved away, and in another moment was gone.

I could scarcely believe what I had seen. Buster sat there looking replete and well-fed, but Tiny had got nothing. For a moment or two Tiny's mouth opened a couple of times, as if he might be saying, *Hey, I'm over here, Mama! You forgot me. What about me?* – but she was no longer there. Then, as if he finally accepted that she'd gone, he kind of retreated and shrank into himself. I felt so sorry for him. Poor little thing, he just kind of sat there, looking miserable. Not so surprising, really – he hadn't been fed; he was still hungry.

I stayed there for a while longer, looking through, and thinking what a remarkable scene it was. As I said, it was like nothing out of my experience, like nothing I'd ever glimpsed before. And I'm not just talking about the basic nature of the creature comforts – well, there weren't any of those – the word *comfort* didn't come into it. For a start, the place was really mucky. And I don't just mean that it was untidy. To be honest, it was truly squalid, absolutely filthy. I'd never seen anything like it. It made you wonder how any baby could be raised in such conditions. Still, it was none of my business. I was a stranger, an onlooker, someone looking in where he really had no right to be. I kept on looking, though, I had to.

Oh, yes, I kept looking. I was hooked. Over the days, before going out and after getting back following some session of sightseeing or wandering the lovely Florence streets, at the slightest provocation I'd be at the shutters, gently, gently easing them open, looking to see if there was anything new to observe, if there had been any developments. I looked in on the family at regular intervals – never leaving them unobserved for long. For one thing I think I'd attuned my ear to the sounds of their living, so that the second that Mama appeared – always making the same bustling, busy little sounds – I became aware of it, and I was there, the shutters opened, peering through the screen, though always, of course, making sure there was no light behind me in my room, so that they'd have no idea that they were being watched.

And the scene hardly changed at all – not in any significant way, anyway. The two of them, Buster and Tiny, seemed all the time to remain almost unmoving when their mother was out and they were alone. And they made very little noise – almost as if they knew that there was no point in carrying on and kicking up a fuss if she wasn't there. It was only at mealtimes, when she was there with them, that they seemed to come alive. And always at those times it was Buster who got all the attention. It was always him. And in a way he made sure of it. When she appeared it was always his voice that was the louder, making sure he got the attention, while poor little Tiny wasn't getting fed at all – at least not on any of the occasions when I was able to look in on them. I thought once or twice that maybe I'd missed something, not been attentive enough, or had been looking in at the wrong time. But I realised that that wasn't the case – that's the way it was developing – the way it had developed. It was Buster – Buster who was getting all his mother's focus – and all the goodies, too. And while he was crying and getting fed, little Tiny was being ignored. Totally. He was there so close to his mother, and desperately wanting to be fed, but she simply took no notice of him. It was just Buster – Mama's boy, her favourite. He was getting it all.

It couldn't go on indefinitely, I thought. While Tiny wasn't getting fed, Buster was thriving. And it showed. Oh, how it showed! You could see the difference in them – it was becoming more apparent with every passing day. Buster was putting on weight, looking really fit and healthy, while his twin looked as if he was wasting away. He was shrinking before my eyes.

And of course I wondered – as you would – whether there was something I could do. Well, something had to be done, I thought – but what? I mean, I was a stranger, an alien in their world, with no real means of communicating. But I couldn't just disregard what was going on in front of my eyes. So, one afternoon when Mama had departed – once again ignoring little Tiny's pleas to be fed – I decided to take action.

Take action, I say. It was perhaps the most pathetic gesture, but I was at a loss. I had no idea what to do for the best – if indeed I could do anything at all.

A day or two earlier, from a nearby supermarket I had bought a pack of biscuits. They were sweet and delicious and at night I enjoyed one or two along with the cup of tea I made with the kettle, tea-bags and milk provided. Now, I got a couple of the biscuits and placed them in a cup. Then I added a little milk and mashed it up a bit.

Holding the cup, I moved back to the window and, as quietly as I could, opened the shutters.

There they were, side by side, Buster and Tiny, one looking vital and healthy, the other pale and fading by the hour.

I looked more closely at the mesh, and its frame. I had to get access to the other side. Then I saw that it wouldn't be any great problem. Running my fingers around the frame I found that it was just a matter of pushing it up – as simple as that. It was on hinges, and finding the opening at the bottom, I gave it a tug. There was a little crack of sound, and then I was lifting it, easing it up.

I lifted it right up, all the time watching the faces of Buster and Tiny. Watching for some signs of some alarm on their hearing me and seeing me, I watched as they just seemed to freeze. What was thrilling, though, is that they were now so much closer. So close that I could reach in and touch them.

There they were, the two of them.

My attention, though, was all on Tiny.

'Oh, Tiny, Tiny,' I whispered softly, ' – it's going to be all right – I've got some dinner here for you.'

With a teaspoon I scooped up a little bit of the milk-soaked biscuit, and carefully, moving so, so slowly, I bent forward and reached through.

'Tiny ... Tiny, open up for me ...' I breathed the words, my voice a little louder, at the same time holding the tip of the spoon as close to his mouth as I could.

Nothing.

'Please – Tiny,' I whispered. 'Please – *eat*. Eat or you'll die. Just eat. *Please, eat ...*'

Nothing. He just didn't respond. *Wouldn't* respond? It was as if he would accept nothing that didn't come from his mother. '*Please,*' I said. '*Please.*' I was holding the little morsel of food so close. He could have taken it, eaten it and it would have helped him, I know, but he didn't move – except to draw back even further. It was as if he was afraid. And why not? Why not be afraid? Of course he was afraid. He must have been terrified.

I mean, who was this stranger who was suddenly invading his home, holding out to him a spoonful of some unaccustomed food?

'*Please, Tiny, please . . .*'

But it was no good. In the end I gave up and drew back. There was no point in persevering. The food, my little offering, my little life-saving offering, was not going to be taken.

'I could have saved you,' I murmured. But there, how often do we get the lesson that some individuals, although offered salvation, simply do not want it.

I gave up all attempts to help after that, my failure. What did I know, I thought? As I said, it was a foreign scene for me, and I was a foreigner there. There I was, like the proverbial bull in the china shop, clueless and blundering around, not knowing what to do for the best. If, indeed, anything could be done. And if it wasn't too late.

Well, yes, it was. Too late. Of course it was, and I had done nothing. I felt totally helpless and ineffectual.

Over the next few days I watched as their lives went on – as Mama came bustling in, bringing food – and Buster, only Buster got fed. And as Buster grew stronger by the day, poor Tiny continued to fade away.

And then, one bright, sunny morning I looked in and saw that Tiny was dead.

He lay there, almost naked in the filth that covered the floor, while beside him Buster, appearing totally unconcerned, ate and throve, while Mama, devoted Mama, came bustling in, bringing to him, her favoured boy, everything good that she could possibly bring.

The following day I looked in and saw that Tiny was now almost disappearing down into the dirt. And as I looked I heard the sound of the mother coming home. Next second she was there, coming in in her usual vital, determined way, goodies on board for Buster, her boy.

And I watched as, to my utter horror, she walked over the filthy floor and actually stood on the body of her dead baby. I could scarcely believe my eyes. She was standing on his corpse, walking on him. Either she simply didn't care, or she was totally unaware of what was beneath her feet. Whatever it was, for her, Tiny had long since ceased to exist.

How swiftly events moved on. It wasn't long before I saw that Tiny had all but disappeared from sight. His little body was hardly visible, and I was sure that had any other stranger come to look in they would not even have known that he was there, that under all the dirt lay the corpse of an innocent, blameless babe. Oh, yes, *I* knew he was there – or rather his sad little remains – but only I was aware of it, I'm sure. As for his mother and his brother, he might never have been.

And taking in the dreadful scene I cried out to her, unable to help myself: 'How could you do this? How could you? You're heartless. You've killed him.'

And at the sudden sound of my voice she turned and looked right at me. It was only the briefest glance, but it was enough. The next moment, taking fright, she whirled and dashed away.

I watched her go. We both did, I and Buster, her little boy, her little chick – her strong, healthy chick. Like me, he watched her departure. His feathers had grown so strongly over the past few days, and I knew it wouldn't be long before he'd be leaving the nest. It wouldn't be long before he'd be following his mother, the plump Florentine pigeon, across the width of the window sill, through the narrow gap between the outside shutter and the wall, and winging out into the warm, Florentine air.

FORGET-ME-NOT

'THAT's the house where Christie lived . . .'

Sandra followed the direction of the young man's pointing finger and saw, through the window, below them, a shabby cul-de-sac.

'The one just at the end,' he said. 'Right next to that factory wall.'

Quickly, Sandra shifted her gaze, but there was only time to catch the briefest glimpse of the drab-looking terrace house before the Tube train – travelling over-ground for this stretch – took them past. The house vanished from sight.

'Who is Christie?' she asked in her New York accent; she was a stranger to England and curious about everything.

'Who *was* Christie,' he corrected her. 'John Reginald Halliday Christie – preferred to be called Reginald, I believe. Oh, he was just a harmless-looking little man who killed – murdered – a number of women. He was hanged for it.'

'Really?' Sandra thought of the very ordinary house she had just seen. 'And he *lived there?*'

'Yes. And committed all the murders there.'

She shivered slightly, in spite of the warm September air.

The young man went on: 'His victims were all female. Most of them were – ' He broke off suddenly, grinning. 'Listen to me,' he said, ' – a fine introduction to London this is for you!'

She laughed. 'No, no, it's fascinating! Anyway, I want to know *everything* – the good *and* the bad.' She paused, then added: 'It's funny, but somehow I never thought of associating London with any kind of gruesome violence like that.'

'Oh, we have our share,' he said, then, changing the subject, asked: 'Have you got a place to stay?'

'Yes, I've booked into a hotel for a while. Just till I can find a room or an apartment . . .'

'That might not be so easy.'

She smiled, undeterred. 'I'll find something. I'll start looking tomorrow. I've got a whole week before I start school.'

Sandra Kesselan, pretty, blonde, twenty-six years old, had come to London from the U.S.A. to teach in the London Education system – just for a year, on an exchange basis. For months she had looked forward to it, and now the actual day of her arrival was here. It was one of the most exciting days of her life.

'The next stop is yours,' the young man said. He had been scribbling on a piece of paper and now, as she stood up, he handed it to her. 'My name and phone number,' he explained. 'Perhaps when you're settled you might give me a ring . . .'

'Thanks. I'll do that.' She stuffed the note into her pocket and picked up her two suitcases. 'You've been a great help. Honestly, I don't know how I'd have managed.'

He was eager to be even more helpful. 'Can you find your way to the hotel?' he asked.

She nodded. 'I got me a street map. I'll get there okay.' The train was slowing. She moved towards the doors. 'Bye. And thanks again.'

He turned to wave a hand. 'Goodbye. Nice to meet you. And don't forget – phone me . . .'

Outside the station she looked at the slip of paper he had given her. *David Hampshire*, she read. Below the name was his telephone number. 'Yeah, maybe I will give him a call,' she said to herself.

With the help of her *A to Z* street guide it was relatively easy to locate the hotel. The room to which she was then shown looked quite cosy and inviting. Left alone, she kicked off her shoes, lit a cigarette and lay back on the bed. She was relaxed. There was no one to drag her into conversation, no one to tell her that she shouldn't smoke; she was wonderfully comfortable and alone. 'But don't get too comfortable, girl,' she told herself. 'Don't get too settled. You've got to go out and find something a little more permanent. And if David was right, that is not going to be easy.' She was not worried, though; the hunting might be fun. And anyway, one thing was certain – she was going to adore her stay in London – absolutely adore it.

David proved to be right. Finding something a little more permanent proved to be very difficult. My God, she thought, it's as bad as New York! It seemed that no matter how swift she was to answer the ads in the papers, or those in the shop windows, she was always just one bit too late; the room or the flat was always gone. But she'd get something, she told herself; she wasn't easily daunted. In the meantime, the hotel made a comfortable haven.

It was during her flat-searching that she found, in a small corner bookshop, the volume on Christie. As soon as she saw the book: *Christie, Mass Murderer*, she remembered her conversation on the train. The book was second-hand and at a ridiculously low price. Sorting out the still strange coins from her purse she handed them, along with the book, to the assistant. 'I'll take it,' she said.

She began to read the book that same afternoon, continuing with it into the evening. And even when she went down to the little café, she took it with her to study over her steak pie and chips.

The story was absolutely fascinating. Christie was known to have killed at least seven women – by strangulation – and then to have secreted their bodies either in the house or the adjoining garden. His wife had been one of the victims, and a young tenant of the house another. Equally horrifying to Sandra was the fact that after killing each of the women he had undressed them and – and ... She closed her eyes tight. The image in her mind was too terrible to bear.

Later, when she took up the book again, she came upon a photograph of the house. The sight of it caused her to catch at her breath. *Ten Rillington Place*, she read ... But was that the name she had seen on the street sign ...? No, surely not. Quickly she flicked through the pages to the appendix. Yes, there it was: *Ruston Close*. *That* was the name she had seen. After Christie's trial and execution the local authorities had – for obvious reasons – renamed the ugly little dead-end street. She remembered suddenly that David had pointed out the house just before she had got off the Tube. With a strange little thrill she realised that *Ruston Close* was very, very near.

That night she found herself thinking more about the house where Christie had lived. And the things that had happened there. Stop it! she admonished herself; she was getting morbid! What she needed was to start work – to meet people, make a few nice friends . . . She thought of David. He had said he'd be glad to hear from her – so maybe she'd give him a ring. Yes, that was a good idea. For some minutes she searched around for the scrap of paper on which he had written his telephone number, but then, meeting with no success, she gave up the attempt. She'd find it later, there was plenty of time. She went back to her reading.

And all at once, there was Christie, staring at her from the page.

He had a thin, rather gaunt aspect. The hair on his domed head was thinning, and the cold, pale eyes that peered out through the steel-rimmed spectacles were merciless. He had been photographed standing in the tiny, untidy garden of his home, standing with his plump smiling wife. Sandra found herself addressing the unfortunate, unattractive victim: 'You poor, poor thing,' she whispered, 'you wouldn't be smiling if you *knew* . . .'

Her first day at school the following Monday was very tiring. But that was to be expected – teaching was never an easy job, no matter what the age of your pupils. Sandra was given a class of eleven year olds – a vital, noisy group that left her, at four o'clock, feeling drained and exhausted. She departed through the school gates with aching feet, a throat sore from constant shouting, and a mouth that was dry and dusty from the chalk-laden air. Reaching Edgware Road Tube station, she got on the train and settled back with a sigh of relief – her first day was over. The feeling of relief was only temporary, though – she'd have to face another day tomorrow, *and* the day after, *and* the day after that. The days stretched before her into infinity. 'Don't worry,' she told herself, 'it's just because you're not used to it. It'll be all right in time ...' And there was another problem, also – the need for a flat of her own. The worry nagged like a toothache. She'd try again this weekend, she decided – really make an all-out effort. There *had* to be something *somewhere*. She gazed from the window, idly noted the stations as they passed by, after Edgware Road came Paddington, then Royal Oak, then Westbourne Park, then Ladbroke Grove, then ... And suddenly *the house* was there – Christie's house – standing forlorn and dirty at the end of the cul-de-sac, shadowed by the tall, grey, ugly chimney. She turned as the train sped past, craning her neck to catch the last little glimpse.

Every day that week she saw the house. Sitting on the train, she found herself counting the stations – almost impatient, just waiting for the street to come in sight. And always, at the end of the street, was the house. But it looked so – innocuous. It was hard to believe that *that* was the scene of so many hideous crimes.

And yet ... there *was something* about the place, that last tired-looking three-story dwelling. Something about the whole street. And then she realised what it was that gave it all that air of – difference: the street was uninhabited. No people walked there, no children played. The windows were dark and empty, some of them boarded up.

In the morning, on the way to school, she couldn't see the house – the train, running on the left tracks, was too far over, affording her no possible view. But on the way back – well, that was a different matter.

Her days at school could be bearable when there was something to look forward to. And Sandra *did* look forward to the house. Each teaching day, with thumping heart and damp palms, she watched, waited for the house to come into view. Soon – she could see – the house was waiting for *her*.

She *needed* something to look forward to at this time. Somehow, her life was becoming increasingly lonesome. It just wasn't that easy to make friends.

For some people it was, but not for Sandra. The warm, satisfying relationships she had envisaged somehow seemed never to materialize. Why was it? she wondered. She *had* tried, too. Though there was, at school, no one with whom she thought she'd really *like* to be friends, she had, even so, made two or three half-hearted attempts to strike up more than the passing acquaintanceship. But her attempts were not very successful, and she was forced to continue with the amusements of her own designing.

Having no television set and no radio, she spent a great deal of her time reading, getting the books from the local library. And she read more on Christie. John Reginald Halliday Christie. What a name! she thought. The syllables just rolled off her tongue – *John . . . Reginald . . . Halliday . . .* Beautiful. But she thought of him now as Reginald – as he had preferred. And she almost felt as if she was beginning to know him. But that was silly, she knew.

One afternoon, returning from school, she looked down at the street and saw workmen moving about. And there was a bulldozer and other machines of demolition! 'My God!' she whispered; then louder: '*They're knocking it down!*' A woman on the opposite seat looked up from her knitting and gave her an odd, uncomprehending glance.

And they *were* knocking it down. The next day on her return, Christie's house was just a pile of rubble, and the workmen were starting on the house next door.

At school in the staff room, one of the young teachers came to her holding out a newspaper. 'Here,' he said, 'you're the one who's always reading about Christie . . .' He pointed to a short column on the back page. Concealing her eagerness, she took the paper from him and read the words. It only told her what she already knew. But why tear it down? she asked herself. The reason given here: *space needed for redevelopment* was just not good enough. It was *Christie's* house. They shouldn't have done it. It just wasn't fair.

It was that same evening that she found the flat. She had stopped at a small shop to buy cigarettes – she was smoking far too much these days – when she saw the card in the window. *Flat to Let*, it said. *Suit young working person. £11 per week*. Yes, she could afford that much, she reckoned. Quickly she made a note of the address, then set off at once to find it.

And now it was hers. She had paid Mr Malaczynski, the Polish landlord, a month's rent in advance and told him that she'd be moving in the very next day. She'd take the day off school, she decided. She didn't feel like going anyway; there was nothing to look forward to anymore.

There were three flats available, the landlord had told her, so she could have her choice. She chose the one on the first floor. At the moment the ground floor flat was occupied by the landlord himself. 'But only for a short time,' he explained. 'I'll be moving to another house this coming weekend.' Then, continuing in his accented English: 'Will you mind being here on your own for a while? It won't be long before the other flats are let.'

'Oh, no,' she had assured him. 'It won't bother me in the least.' Nor would it. She had her own place – at last. Nothing would bother her now.

The next day she paid her hotel bill and moved into the flat. Now at last, she had finally arrived. She stood in her bed-sitting room and looked around her. She had just the two rooms – this one, which was fairly large – and a smaller kitchen next door. The bathroom was on the floor above, and she'd have to share it with the incoming tenant – whoever that might turn out to be. But it didn't matter. The flat was hers. It was small, but it was *hers*.

All the walls were a sort of greyish white. Not attractive. But she'd repaint them in time, she thought. For the present they'd look all right with a bit of colour added: a few pictures, ornaments. It was going to be fun shopping for things. She could make the place really attractive. Though it was by no means perfect – particularly to a sophisticated New Yorker – it had endless possibilities.

After she had unpacked, she spent a long time arranging her few things, trying, futilely, to add a touch of her own personality. It couldn't be done, she discovered – not in a day. It could only come with *living* there.

In the course of her sorting-out, she came across David Hampshire's name and phone number. She put the scrap of paper carefully between the leaves of her address book. Maybe she would invite him round for supper, she thought – but not just yet; not till she was well and truly settled.

She stayed up late that night, cleaning and scrubbing. There was so much to be done when moving into a new place. Eventually, totally exhausted, she got into bed and gazed about her. The room didn't look quite so bare, anyway. On the wall nearest the foot of the bed she had pinned a postcard-size reproduction of Murillo's *Peasant Boy Leaning on a Sill*. She had bought the small print at the National Gallery during her first days in London. She loved the soft, muted tones of the picture and the boy's wide, happy smile. Next to it, making something of a contrast, she had displayed the photograph of Christie and his wife. She had torn the picture from her book.

Lying there, very comfortable, she made vague plans about what she would do with the flat. She'd have to make a list of all the things that were needed – and there were so many things – still, it would come, gradually. Sighing, feeling tired but happy, she switched off the small lamp and turned over to go to sleep.

Four hours later, she was still wide-awake. In spite of her great exhaustion from the hectic day, sleep just would not come. Shifting restlessly, she was aware of the dawn lightening the pale curtains at the windows. She gave a groan of exasperation – she *had* to get some rest. At last, sometime after, she drifted off.

She awoke hours later, having slept right through the strident ringing of her alarm clock. She saw with a shock that the time was after eleven! It was no good going in to school now. She'd phone in and explain. Anyway, she remembered that next week was half-term holiday; it hardly seemed worth going in – not just for those few remaining hours.

She made good use of the rest of the day. After her phone call to the headmistress she went out shopping. She bought china, saucepans, cutlery – those items necessary for the furnishing of a home. And that evening she cooked supper for herself – no more eating out at cafés. The meal was a pleasant – though somewhat lonely – affair, and she experienced a real sense of achievement. After this, she washed the dishes, then read for a few hours.

She wasn't sure when the idea came to her – or whether it had been there all the time, just waiting to be acknowledged. But it was the picture of Christie that actually set it. It had to be. For one thing, his eyes followed her all the time. And every time she looked up from her book, he was looking at her. She had to go there. She had to go to the place where he, Reginald, had lived and breathed – and killed.

It was very late when she left the house. The last Tubes had gone, and only the occasional car disturbed the silence of the dingy street. Her footsteps echoing on the pavements, she walked in the general direction of Ruston Close. She had consulted her *A to Z*, and knew exactly which way to go.

And suddenly it was there.

She came upon it at once, and the shock of the expected discovery almost took her breath away. Her heart beating wildly, she stood at the entrance to the close, gazing before her at the familiar shape of the chimney, only slightly darker than the dark night sky.

Everything was so quiet. On her right a cinema poster flapped against a wall – it was the only sound in the stillness.

Nothing else moved. Completely deserted, the *cul-de-sac* stretched dark and forbidding before her, the windows of the remaining houses like dead, blind eyes.

She found that she was holding her breath. She exhaled, slowly. The atmosphere – there was an atmosphere – poured over her. The place had its own feeling; and it reached out to her as she stood there on the street corner, clutching at her with soft, grasping fingers, drawing her in.

She tried to walk softly, but the cold wind that swirled around the corner followed her, buffeting so that her raincoat flapped noisily against her legs. No moon or stars were visible; the old street was all dark greyness, almost at one with the sky. And then she had reached the end. Standing beneath the chimney, she peered into the gloom of the place where Christie's house had stood.

As she gazed, shivering, the moon appeared from behind a cloud. All at once the scene was lit up before her, and she saw in the sudden light that the house wall on the right – the one adjoining the factory wall – had not, like all the others, been torn down. It stood there still. And there, yawning in the wall-like grotesque mouths – were the fireplaces. *Christie's* fireplaces. Scraps of torn, discoloured wallpaper still adhered to some of the surfaces around.

Crossing over the rubble, she touched the wall with the tips of her fingers. Then, gaining courage, she laid her whole hand, flat, against it. Underneath her palm the wallpaper was brittle and flaking. After a moment, she took hold of a piece of the paper . . . and pulled . . . There was a loud tearing noise, and a strip about nine inches long and four inches wide came away in her grasp. She had taken the piece from an area just above her own head. It might well, she thought, be an area that Reginald had actually touched, have actually leaned his own domed, balding head against. Carefully she eased the strip – it was made from several thicknesses – into a roll, then tucked it away inside her coat.

Arriving back at the downstairs entrance to her flat, she let herself in and climbed the stairs. The silence was as complete as that which she had just left. It would be even more silent when the landlord left tomorrow . . .

In her room, she unrolled the paper and laid it flat on the table. She was pleased. It made a nice souvenir. Then, later, she pasted it onto the greying wall, just to the right of the gas fire, slightly above the level of her head. She studied the result judiciously for some moments, then, with a smile of satisfaction, climbed into bed.

But once again, rest did not come easily. It was only after tossing and turning for a very long time that she eventually dropped off into a fitful, uneasy sleep – a sleep disturbed by dreams that kept her peace at bay.

Next day she awoke very late. Still, it being Saturday, this time it didn't matter. She lay in bed looking at Reginald's wallpaper. It really stood out against the dull background of the painted wall. The paper had been so affected by dirt and age that it was difficult to determine what its original colour had been. Probably blue, she decided at last; blue with some kind of small design on it. Flowers? Yes, perhaps, but she couldn't possibly identify what species. She gazed at the paper for a long, long time. Yes, definitely flowers, she decided, and the background most certainly blue. It had probably been quite pretty when newly bought. She felt rather smug; for one thing, she hadn't remembered tearing off such a large piece. With a last look, she turned over and went back to sleep.

She stayed up very late again on Saturday night, then slept well into the afternoon of the following day. She awoke about two o'clock, feeling sluggish and heavy-headed, not feeling like getting up at all. Anyway, there was nothing she had planned to do, no shopping could be done, and there was no one she had planned to see, so the day – or what was left of it – was her own. She could do exactly as she pleased. Later on, she thought, she'd get up and make herself a snack – something light – maybe a soft-boiled egg. But she wasn't really hungry. Propping up the pillows behind her head, she sat up, lit a cigarette and reached for her book. It was a new one from the library, all about famous trials. There was a particularly interesting chapter on Reginald.

She forgot about eating until it was quite late. Hardly worth it now, she thought. She'd just have a cup of coffee and a biscuit.

As she waited for the water to boil, her thoughts went back to her own home in New York City – the home she had shared with her parents and her four sisters. My God! she thought, if my mother could see me now she'd have a fit! There had always been so much emphasis placed on regular habits – regular meals and regular sleeping times. But Sandra had wanted this independence, this solitude. They were all part of her reasons for coming to this strange city.

All around her, the house was as silent as a tomb. There was no longer even the soft, considerate movements of the landlord to disturb the stillness. He had left the day before and until the new tenants moved in she would be completely alone.

Having no intention of going out, there seemed little purpose in getting dressed, so when the coffee was made she carried it back to bed. Over the rim of the cup she gave a casual glance at the strip of wallpaper. Then she looked harder, studying intently the size, the shape and the colour of the piece. It seemed different somehow. But how? And *how could* it? No. It was silly; such a thing just wasn't possible. She stared at it, unblinking. But it was true. It was different. The piece of paper had grown bigger.

She hardly stirred from the house all that week, except to go to the shop for cigarettes and the odd items of food; not so much for the latter, as she had found that her appetite had decreased considerably. And there was the silence of the house. It was complete. She began to wish that she owned a television set, a radio or maybe a record-player. It was as if the silence, unchecked, seemed to gain in potency and, along with Reginald's wallpaper, grew with each passing day.

Friday came, then Saturday, then Sunday, and then Monday loomed up over her head, threatening, and suddenly she knew that she just could not face the prospect of school that day. She couldn't face the children in the classrooms, the idle talk with the other teachers during the breaks between sessions. She'd just have to telephone in again, tell them she was sick. They'd understand.

She got to the telephone on the floor and started to dial the school's number. Halfway through she stopped, replaced the receiver, then turned and went back up the stairs to her room. There was no need to call them, anyway, she rationalized later: *they* would call *her* as soon as they discovered her absence. But then, in a moment the thought came to her: How could they? No one at the school was aware of her new address or telephone number. She hadn't even told her parents, she realised – in fact, she had not even *written* to her parents since before leaving the hotel. Only Mr Malaczynski, the landlord, knew of her whereabouts, and he didn't really count.

Monday went by in silence. Tuesday morning came. She forced herself to get up, and began to get ready for school. There was a pounding in her head and a constricted feeling as if her skull was being slowly tightened. The pain was throbbing. She sat down on the chair and pulled on her boots. The wallpaper had spread inches during the night.

She was fully dressed. It was time to go. But the thought of facing all those people – the teachers, the children – all those questions that would have been asked: 'Has anyone seen or heard from Miss Kessellan?' 'Does anyone know her address . . . ?' And the questions and the comments when she *did* get there: 'Where *were* you . . . ? What happened . . . ? You should have let us know. Are you ill? Why didn't you telephone . . . ?' All those looks, all those words . . .

It was the thought of the looks, the faces, the words that

settled the matter. She took off all her clothes, threw them over the back of the chair and got back into bed.

She was awakened some hours later by someone tapping at her door. She got out of bed and slipped on her dressing gown. 'Who is it?' she called.

The landlord's voice came to her, the Polish accent strong: 'It's Mr Malaczynski.'

Sandra opened the door a few inches. 'Yes, what is it?'

He smiled broadly at her. 'It's just that – ' he broke off, gazing at her with concern. 'Are you all right?'

'Yeah, I'm fine. Why?'

'You . . . you don't look well. Are you ill?'

She felt a growing sense of impatience under the well-meaning questions. 'Of course I'm not ill. What did you want?' Her tone was slightly sharp.

'I'm very sorry,' he said, wilting a little under the edge on her voice. 'I just wanted to tell you that if you hear footsteps above, there is no need to be frightened. Mr Robertson, the new tenant, is moving in today. He is an old man. He won't cause you worry with rock-and-roll music.' He smiled again, trying to break through the impatient, cold exterior she presented. He added lamely: 'He will be here soon.'

There seemed to be nothing more to say. They looked at each other for a few seconds, and Sandra, trying to ease the warmth into her voice, said: 'Thank you, very much.' He smiled back at her, grateful. 'Thank you,' he answered and moved toward the stairs.

When he had gone from sight, she closed the door and walked over to the mirror. She stood there, gazing at her reflection.

She certainly didn't look one hundred per cent, she had to admit. Her face was drawn and pale, and the lines around her eyes made her look older than her twenty-six years. And her hair needed washing, she observed. It hung limp, lifeless and uncombed to her shoulders. She'd do it tomorrow, she thought.

About seven o'clock she heard the arrival of the new tenant; she could hear the soft movements of his feet as he moved around on the floor above. What was his name? Robertson? Yes, that's what Malaczynski had said. Perhaps they could be friends. It might be nice to talk to someone. Just a little talk. Just something to relieve the silence . . .

The days went by. And each day was like the one before. The only way of actually seeing that time had progressed was by watching the wallpaper. It looked different each time she awoke. Always it grew during the night – some nights more than others. The silence grew with it.

The arrival of Mr Robertson upstairs had made no difference to the house at all. It was just as quiet. Other people were plagued with neighbours who played their radios and their records too loudly – not so Sandra. Mr Robertson had none of these and lived as silently as she. The only evidence of his presence was the soft sound of his feet as he occasionally moved about the room. The faint noises did nothing to alleviate the stillness. They just seemed to emphasize it. The stillness grew louder all the time, and the paper seemed to feed upon the stillness. Yes! *That* was what was happening. She suddenly realised. Although normally silent – the house – throughout the day – it was at night when the silence became absolute, so strong, so complete, that it was almost tangible. And it was during the night that the wallpaper seemed to grow at such an alarming rate . . . All the plans for transforming the ugly little flat into something that was truly her own were now forgotten. They had ceased to be important. Sandra sat on the bed, a cup of cold, untouched coffee in her hand, looking about her. What was happening to her? She didn't understand it. How long had she been here in this room – three weeks? – four? She shivered violently. The room was cold, and she had run out of shillings for the meter. She'd have to go down to the shop to get some more. Sighing, she put down her cup and began to get dressed.

As she moved quietly about, the idea came into her mind

that she should buy herself a radio. She had seen some inexpensive transistors not too far away. And she could just about afford it from the little she had left of her savings. The idea added impetus to her movements and she finished dressing quickly, anxious to be out. As she turned toward the door she caught sight of her reflection. Hurriedly she crossed to the sink and splashed cold water on her face. (The soap she had bought on her first day lay unused, still in its wrapper.) Then she raked a hand through her tangled hair.

First of all she got the supply of shillings. She got them from the bank – two pounds' worth. Now, she thought, she'd get that radio.

It was while she stood outside the entrance to the bank, wondering which way to go, that the weakness came over her. Suddenly she felt that her legs were about to give way. Her knees wobbled, she thought she was about to fall and she clutched at the wall for support.

'Are you feeling all right, love . . .'

She turned at the soft voice and tried to focus on the man who stood there, leaning toward her. For a moment she stared at herself, mirrored in the lenses of his steel-rimmed glasses, and then she turned, swinging away on her unsteady feet.

Back in her room, she collapsed, gasping, on the bed. It was a long time before she gathered the strength to undress and get in between the sheets. On the wall, Reginald's paper was enormous.

Later, feeling calm again, she lay back and studied the paper. It had now spread in all directions, reaching out to the right as far as the mirror and on the left almost as far as the shabby wardrobe. But she was no longer shocked by it. It had long since ceased to amaze her in any way. She looked at it now with acceptance, interest. After all, there was nothing she could do about it.

With the change in its size, the wallpaper had also changed in quality – or rather than that – it appeared to be *newer*. In fact it looked brand-new now. She wondered how she could ever have had to *decide* on its colour; it was quite obviously blue, a rather pretty pale blue. Likewise, the flowers that dotted its surface were now easily identifiable. They were the prettiest forget-me-nots, always among her favourite flowers. She thought: So goddamn *English*, too, and found herself smiling. The wallpaper was like some fungus – a creeping, thriving, rapacious, beautiful, beautiful fungus.

After a while, she got out of bed, lit the gas fire and put on some water for coffee. Nervously she stretched out a hand and touched the paper. It felt slightly damp, yet the other walls – the grey ones – were quite dry under her fingers. Gently she tried to insert a fingernail under the edge of the paper, but she couldn't do it – the paper was too firmly fixed. With the second try – in a different spot – she only succeeded in breaking her nail. Without any sense of disappointment, she picked up her coffee and moved back to the bed.

The school, her job as a teacher, her home in New York – all seemed to be disconnected somehow. None of it was real. Not anymore. These were the only things that were real: this room, and this silence. And the wallpaper. Reginald's forget-me-not wallpaper.

The paper had spread so far now. It had reached the far end of the wall and was beginning to turn the corner. There seemed to be no pattern to its actual movement – it just seemed to move, slowly creeping, spreading – rather like some spilled liquid on a polished surface. Some areas of the wall would be left bare, she noticed, and then, later, she would see that they had been filled in. The paper was relentless and very, very thorough.

Even the little peasant boy was not safe.

She had pinned the postcard up on the wall far away from the paper, and even though the mass of paper had not yet reached it, she could see that the lovely little picture had now become infected. It had started with just a tiny little dot of blue down in one corner. She had noticed it one morning – her eyes seemed to be drawn to it – a little spot that had surely not been in the original. She knew what was happening. The little peasant boy did not, though, and – like Mrs Christie in the photograph – he smiled his smile, unaware of the nearness of the evil. Unconcerned, he continued to lean on the sill, his tanned, peasant boy's face beaming, while the forget-me-nots grew up around him. Sandra thought the picture was prettier. It's a pity, she thought, that Murillo couldn't be here to see it. Looking towards the photograph of Reginald and his wife, she was not surprised to see that it remained exactly as before. No forget-me-nots grew on that one. Looking closer, she saw that the paper was spreading *underneath* it.

Nothing was staying the same. Nothing. Even the quality of the silence was changing. Looking toward the window she saw the reason why. Snow was falling, thick and fast, the great soft shapes tumbling against the pane, settling. They fell without sound, insulating her more completely against the outside world.

And suddenly, she began to grow afraid. It had to stop. Everything had to stop. She had to *do something*. She didn't know what she was afraid of, but the fear grew, unexplainable, threatening, as if at any moment it would engulf her. She knew at once that she had to see someone, talk to someone. But who? There was no one she knew. Not Mr Robertson; she had only glimpsed him on the stairs on two or three occasions. He had nodded to her, smiling, a slow-moving, sad old man of seventy-odd. He couldn't help. Who, then?

David. David Hampshire. She saw his face before she thought of his name; that nice young man who had been so helpful on the Tube that day of her arrival.

She took the piece of paper bearing his phone number and snatched a handful of coins from the shelf. Then, throwing on a coat and slippers, she went downstairs. Carefully, her hands trembling, she dialled his number.

'Hello . . . ?' There was his voice.

'Hello . . . David?' She paused, then added quickly: 'This is Sandra Kesselan.'

'Who?'

Oh, God, he'd forgotten. 'I'm the girl you met on the Tube,' she said. 'The American girl.' She could hear herself almost whimpering. 'Don't you remember . . . ?'

And then she heard the smile in his voice as recollection returned.

'Oh, yes!' he said. 'Yes, of course, I remember. How are you? Have you been okay?'

She began to blurt out her need for help. She had not meant to do this; she had meant to ask him to come round to see her – to tell him then – to do it more – casually. But somehow the desperation inside her had taken over, and she was pleading with him.

'Help me. You've got to help me!'

'What's wrong?' he asked, his voice sounding heavy with concern.

'I don't know – I don't know – I don't know . . .'

'Right, listen,' he said, forcing the calmness into the situation. 'Tell me where you are. I'll drive round straight-away.' He took up a pencil. 'Give me your address.'

She was almost incoherent, but he managed to write down the address she gabbled out.

'I'll be there in fifteen minutes.'

'Yes, yes! Please hurry . . . Please *hurry!*' And she was gone.

David heard the click of the receiver and put the phone down. As he reached for his coat he looked at the address he had scribbled on the notepad. He stopped, gazing at it. What was she doing? Was she was having some kind of joke with him? *Some joke* on a night like this. He screwed the paper into a ball and tossed it into the wastebasket. It didn't make sense, he thought, and he was in no mood for games. There was no longer any such address as 10, *Rillington Place*.

Reaching her room, Sandra ran in and closed the door behind her. While she had been out the wallpaper had spread even further. Almost three walls were covered now, and the peasant boy had been completely wiped out. Reginald continued to smile.

Fifteen minutes, David had told her. Fifteen minutes. She could hold out for fifteen minutes. It wasn't very long. Not too long. She could try counting them off – that might help. Count the seconds: one, two, three, four, five, six, seven ... She closed her eyes, shutting out the forget-me-nots that grew all around her. Eight ... nine ... ten ... Now the silence was getting in the way. Where was she? Eight ... nine ... ten ... eleven ... She tried to shut her ears to the silence, but it was no good. It got through. Whatever you did it got through. Make some coffee, she told herself – make some coffee and smoke a cigarette, do *something*. Act naturally ...

The paper had crept onto the fourth wall now. It was moving faster than ever. She hurried to the kitchen, lit the gas under the kettle. That's it – be steady – be calm. Get the jar of coffee – don't spill any. One spoonful ... sugar ... milk ready ... the wallpaper had now gotten into the kitchen, too. There were forget-me-nots everywhere. Take no notice of it. Don't look. Ignore it. David will be here soon. Everything will be all right then. You can wait till then. He won't be long now. The water's boiling. The sound of the steam and the gas are the only sounds. Turn off the gas, pour on the water. Silence. The coffee's made. Add the milk. Sip it, sip it slowly. Concentrate ... concentrate ... She looked at the clock. Half an hour had gone by since she had called David! Where could he be? What had happened to him? Why wasn't he here? Fifteen minutes, he had told her. It was over half an hour ... She sipped at the coffee. It was stone cold, and she put it down in disgust. She moved from the kitchen, back into the larger room, walking slowly, forcing her way through the silence. The silence was like the sea, and it was rising, moment by moment. Reginald liked the silence. He smiled into it from his forget-me-not heaven.

Would David *never* come? But yes! He was *here! At last!* The gentle tap at her door had taken her completely by surprise. She pressed herself against the silence, pushing a way through. She got to the door, opened it. She saw the thin face, the smile, and the blue eyes behind the glasses. She spun, and the sweet, sweet forget-me-not fungus lurched, reaching out. The whole room was blue now, quivering in silence. Then the man spoke. After a second, the silence itself was shattered.

'I wonder if I could borrow a little milk?' the man on the landing had said, holding out an empty cup. 'I've just moved in downstairs . . .' The girl, dirty, emaciated, her tangled hair hanging about her face, just stood there in the open doorway, staring at him dumbly from wide, frightened eyes. He smiled at her, adding: 'My name is Reg,' and suddenly she screamed. Her voice echoed in the quiet house – the sound of something in pain. The screams continued, the loudness cutting into the snowbound silence.

When the screaming stopped, her mouth went on moving, opening and closing like the mouth of a ventriloquist's dummy.

OUR LAST NANNY

M UMMY says we won't have another nanny. Not after Janie. She was the last one – Janie, I mean. But it isn't really a *nanny* that I want, anyway. They're just for babies, and I'm eight – last July. I'd just like somebody who can take you out a bit – round those places where children can't go on their own. Those places are always the most fun, I think. But Mummy says no. No more nannies. So now it's all boring again. I wish Janie was back. We had some good times then.

I shouldn't talk about Janie; I know Mummy wouldn't like me to. She says I've got to forget all about her – to put her out of my head. Whenever I do mention Janie my mother goes all quiet for a minute and then starts talking about something else. I do try. I mean, I do try to 'Put her out of my head', but you can't always do that, can you? I mean, not when it's *there*. You can't stop yourself thinking things, can you? – or remembering things – even if you don't want to. Anyway, I don't think I want to forget Janie. She was a lot of good fun. And there wasn't anybody else around to have fun with. Oh, yes, there was Rick, my brother, but boys are so boring most of the time. And Mummy was always so busy. See, that's how we came to get Janie – because of Mummy's busyness. Mummy always had so much to do, and I suppose she just couldn't spend all her time looking after us. I don't know where my father was. He was always away somewhere. Well, I don't remember him being there at the time, so he must have been away somewhere. So it was just Mummy, Rick and me.

My mother is a writer. She writes books and things like that. Nothing for children. Just for grown-ups. All very boring stuff. We lived in this big house out in the country, all surrounded by fields and trees and streams and things like that. There's just

houses and streets here in the city, with sparrows and pigeons.
I hate it. But there you saw everything. All kinds of things that
you wouldn't dream of. And Janie knew all the best places to
look.

Janie wasn't with us very long – but, you know, I can
remember her so clearly. Yet it was simply ages ago. I was at
least five. Perhaps I was even six. Yes, I was six: I can remember
because Janie was at Rick's party on his fourth birthday. And
that was a lot of fun too. Oh, it was so much nicer when Janie
was with us.

Before Janie came Mummy used to get cross a lot of the
time – so it seemed, anyway. When she had to stop working to
get lunch for us or something she'd really get impatient. Or if
one of us got into trouble when we should have known better –
things like that. And we never seemed to go anywhere: I mean,
not really get taken anywhere. And we weren't allowed to go
wandering off on our own – not far anyway, not far from the
house. We had to stay around. There were all those fields and
things and we couldn't go out in them. School-time wasn't so
bad, but the holidays were really boring. Just hanging around
that big old house and playing in the garden. I mean, there's
a limit to what you can do in a garden, isn't there? And all the
time Mummy would be tapping away at her typewriter, and
if you interrupted her at the wrong time she'd get all irritable,
and blame you if she made a mistake. And sometimes, even
when I did get the idea to go off to explore somewhere on my
own it never worked out. Rick would always see me sneaking
off and he'd call out. Then if I tried to creep off without him
he'd just yell and yell his silly head off. 'Take me with you,
Carolyn,' he'd say. And I'd say, 'No,' so he'd say, 'All right, then,
I'll tell Mummy you're going off.' He would, too. He'd run
indoors and the next minute there Mummy'd be, leaning out
of the window, saying I was not to go off, and I was not to
torment Rick, and – you know – how could she expect to get
any work done with us two kicking up such a fuss. And she'd
end up telling me, 'Now do be a good girl, Carolyn, and don't

let me have to speak to you again.' Then she'd go back to her typewriter and those deadlines and things she used to moan about. I don't know. Anyway, as I said, it was all very, very boring. Until Janie came, that is. She changed all that.

Janie was this big sort of country girl with red cheeks and big hands. Everything about her seemed big, in a way. Her nose, her mouth, her eyes and ears. I make it sound as if she was ugly, but she wasn't at all. She was quite pretty, really. I *remember* her as pretty. Anyway, I don't think I could ever love anyone who was ugly, and I loved Janie.

Janie came because Mummy had to have help, and right from the very start we loved her – Rick and I. She was with us all day long. And at night she slept in the room next to the nursery. So she was the first thing we saw in the mornings and the last thing we saw before we went to sleep. Even when Mummy came up to kiss us goodnight and tuck us in Janie would come after and tell us a little story. She knew so many stories. I never met anyone in my whole life who knew so many stories. I think she came from Wiltshire, or one of those places like that. And just before she came to us she'd been living somewhere in Africa. I was very glad about the Africa thing because for one thing it would stop my friend Frances from keeping on about her nanny, who only came from the Isle of Wight. Janie said she'd been in Africa living with a family there and looking after two little boys. She used to tell us stories about the little boys, and in the end we almost felt we knew them. It was sad, though, too, because the boys died – both of them. Well, after all, they *were* in Africa, a strange, far-away land, and everyone knows you can get all kinds of diseases in foreign countries and places like that. We always had almost to beg her to tell us much about the boys, because really she didn't like talking about them. Well, it upset her; you could see that – she'd loved them so much, and she was heartbroken when they died. Mind you, she told us lots of happy stories too. And exciting ones – real adventures. And she told us about how it was in Africa.

I never minded going to bed when Janie was with us. She was a godsend. That's what Mummy said. When Janie came, Mummy hardly ever got cross. She was able to get on with her writing work and we never ever bothered her. I heard Mummy say to Janie once, 'Janie, you're a godsend. I don't know what we'd do without you.' And *we* used to tell Janie that too, afterwards, Rick and me. 'You're a godsend, Janie,' we used to say to her. 'A godsend, that's what you are.' Well, she was. I can picture her now, sitting on my bed as she told us a story. (She took it in turns: one night she'd sit on my bed, the next night on Rick's.) She always looked so big. But it was a nice, cuddly kind of bigness. Mummy used to say she didn't know how on earth Janie could stay so well – she didn't eat enough to satisfy a sparrow. But she did – stay well, I mean. It was true, too; she never seemed to have much appetite – mind you, Rick and I were sometimes glad about this because we'd always get to have some of the things she didn't want. And I was always hungry. Rick used to say he was, too, but boys will say that just for something to say.

As I said, Janie had the room next to the one that we had. Really, it was practically like being in the same room, because she never closed her door, so we always knew that she was near in case we ever wanted anything in the night. And once when there was a storm we got into her enormous bed with her until the storm was over. And we stayed all night. Janie just let us stay there when we fell asleep. The next morning we woke up, surprised to find where we were, until we remembered how we got there. Janie just laughed and said something like: 'Don't you make a habit of it, you children, now.' But she was never cross with us. A couple of times, too, I went and got into her bed even when there wasn't a storm – maybe because I couldn't get to sleep very well. She'd say all soothey things and I'd go right off just like that. Then in the morning I'd wake up in my own bed. Rick went to her once or twice too, but that was usually because he was afraid of something, some stupid dream or something, but then, he was a boy. I was never frightened. Not really, anyway, not when Janie was there. Janie . . . Janie . . . Janie . . . Oh, Janie, I still don't know why she went – or where.

She came to us in the early spring. I think it was spring. I can't be sure of the exact time, because it was long ago, but I remember the three of us all going out on the day after she arrived. We spent the morning in her room, watching her as she arranged all her own things there. She didn't seem to have many things, and I remember feeling sorry for her, and I offered her my doll that I got two Christmases before, but she didn't take it. No, but she picked me up and kissed me, and said I was a sweet child, or something like that, and I knew right then that I was going to love her and love her and love her. Of course, Rick had to come round then to be kissed as well, though he didn't offer her anything. But she kissed him just the same. She was like that.

It was after all her clothes and other things were put away that she took us out for a walk. Yes, that's how I know it was spring; there were buttercups out. Yes, and celandines and daisies and those flowers like that. She knew the names of all of them. I don't think there was anything she didn't know about nature and growing things and living things and all those things. She always knew where to look for nests and where to look for badgers' earths and rabbits' burrows.

I picked some flowers that afternoon, I remember, and on the way home they wilted and I got tired of carrying them. I wanted to throw them away, but Janie said no, I had picked them, so I must look after them. And if I didn't love them enough to carry them then I should have left them in the ground where they were. But she never said it in an unkind way. She said it in a way that I understood. I must have – I can still remember it.

We had lots of outings in the fields and the woods. We learned something new every day. Mummy said she had never seen us look so healthy and that it was all due to Janie. It was, too.

Then, of course, things had to start going wrong. Why *then*? Why couldn't they have gone wrong at some other time? No, oh no, they had to start just when she was with us. It spoilt it all. And it just got worse. I felt sorry for Janie, and I was afraid that she'd get fed up and leave us. I was afraid that she might think we always had that kind of trouble. I mean, how could she know it had never happened before? I've only thought of this lately – I didn't at the time – but perhaps one of the reasons she's gone is because she got upset. I know she was upset. She must have been.

Anyway – she hadn't been with us very long when it started. At the time I didn't know anything *had* started – not then; it was only later that I came to realise.

We were out in the fields. We'd been for a very long walk and Janie had shown us all kinds of things. It was very hot and we'd been out for hours and hours. We were so tired, and we lay down in the grass, I remember, all three of us. I think Janie must have fallen asleep quite soon; she started to make a faint little funny snoring sound, like some grown-ups do, the air whistling slightly as it came out of her wide nostrils. Rick was lying down near her. He had a magnifying glass – it was new – and he was examining the grass and the ants and things. After a while I turned over and closed my eyes against the sun. It was so peaceful and comfortable.

The next thing I remember is waking up very suddenly at the sound of Rick's voice. He was saying, 'Oh! Oh!' very loudly – as if something had hurt him and frightened him. I sat up, and saw Janie wake up at the same moment. Rick was rubbing his leg. 'What's the matter?' I asked. 'You made me jump.'

He was nearly crying (mind you, he was only little), though he was trying to be brave; I could see it in his mouth – it was all quivery. It was like he wouldn't let himself cry. Janie put her arms around him and cuddled him.

'What is it, darling?' she said. 'Tell Janie all about it.'

Rick went on rubbing his leg. 'Something bit me,' he said.

'I think it was a grasshopper. I saw it on my leg and I knocked it off.'

Well, everyone knows you don't get grasshoppers that early in the year, and anyway, even if you did, they don't bite. I told him so.

'It was!' he said. 'I saw it!' Of course he didn't believe me. He had to ask Janie. 'It could be a grasshopper, couldn't it, Janie?'

Janie didn't know what to answer, you could see. Anyway, she got round it by saying, 'Let's have a look at your leg,' or something like that.

He *had* been bitten. There was a little red, bloody spot on his leg. He scratched at it.

'No, don't do that,' Janie said, and she took her clean white handkerchief and dabbed at the spot. 'Don't scratch it,' she said. 'Just leave it, and it'll be all right.'

I don't think it could have hurt that much, anyway, because when we got home he went to tell Mummy about it looking proud. He told her, too, that a grasshopper had done it. Of course she told him there were no grasshoppers about at this time of year. Of course she did.

That night, while he was asleep, Rick got bitten again. It was such bad luck, I thought. But it was worse this time, because it wasn't just one bite but quite a lot of them. I asked him if he remembered being bitten. He said no, but he thought he'd had a bad dream that nearly woke him up. He showed the bites to Mummy and Janie, and they both agreed that something must have flown in through the window, or else whatever it was he'd brought it back with him from the fields in his clothes. Mummy said, 'Well, if you will roll around in the grass and the hedges you must expect to get bitten or stung, darling.' She was nice when she said it.

And that Janie – oh, she was nice too. Do you know that for supper that night she made a big cream jelly, just because it was Rick's favourite. It really was, too. After his own helping he ate Janie's as well. She wasn't hungry. It was funny, even Rick ate more than Janie did sometimes. That day she didn't even touch her potatoes or greens, and she only nibbled at her meat. Mummy said she had given up worrying whether Janie was getting enough to eat – obviously she was as she always looked so well.

And again that night poor Rick got bitten. When he awoke in the morning his legs were all covered with funny-looking lumps, and there were smudges of blood on his skin and on the sheets.

Mummy and Janie stripped the bed right down and got new sheets and blankets. Then, before they put them on they looked really closely at the mattress – in all the corners – to make sure there were no *things* hiding there. But there was nothing, nothing at all.

Rick didn't want to go to sleep that night. He was afraid. He didn't say he was afraid, but I could tell he was. You could see. Janie tried to cheer him up and said that if he got into bed like a good boy she'd give him a surprise. He went then.

After we were both in bed, and after Mummy had kissed us good night, Janie came in. I couldn't wait to see what the surprise was. It turned out that she could do tricks. And they were really marvellous. I watched as she took a coin in her hand and waved her other hand over it. The coin just seemed to vanish. Then she leaned down and seemed to take it from behind Rick's ear. It was so exciting. Rick felt behind his ear to see if he could find some more money there. He didn't realise it was just a trick. I did, of course.

After finding a penny behind my ear, then finding a sixpence behind her own ear, she started to make them drop from her mouth and her nose. They fell into her palm. It seemed that it was really magic. Rick believed it was. Oh, that Janie! She was so clever! I think she could do anything.

Next morning, Rick's legs were worse and now the funny bite-things were on his arms and chest as well. Mummy looked at him, standing over his bed for a long time. Then she went to phone the doctor.

When the doctor had been and gone I asked Mummy what

was wrong with Rick. She said the doctor didn't really know. I'd never seen Mummy look quite like that before; she looked really worried.

I went up to see Rick as he lay in bed. I walked into the room very softly, just in case he was asleep. He wasn't. 'Hello, Rick.' I whispered it. He just turned his head and looked at me. He used to be smiling all the time, but he wasn't smiling today. He seemed sort of sad, and somehow – smaller . . . I don't know.

'I feel funny, Caro,' he said. His voice was little too.

'You'll soon be all right,' I told him to cheer him up. 'Sometimes things have got to get worse before they can get better.' I'd heard Janie say that once or twice.

'I keep dreaming about those grasshoppers,' he said.

'What grasshoppers?' I said.

'Like that one in the field that time. The one that bit me. Only now there's lots of them. I've seen them hopping round on my bed in the night.'

'I thought you said you were dreaming,' I said.

'Yes,' he said, 'Mummy says I must be. But it's so real. I get scared, Caro.'

'Well, you get bad dreams when you're ill,' I told him. 'Everybody does.' It's true, you do. 'You should have had my dreams when I had the measles,' I said.

He didn't say anything to that, but just started on about the grasshoppers again.

'They're really big,' he said, and he held his hands about two inches apart. 'As big as that.'

'You can't get grasshoppers as big as that,' I said. 'Grasshoppers are little things.'

I tried, but I couldn't cheer him up. When I left him he was crying, so I told Mummy. She asked me if I'd been upsetting him, and of course I hadn't. I mean it wasn't me.

From that night on Mummy went round and made sure that all our windows were closed so that nothing could get in during the night – if something was getting in. But nothing made any difference. Every morning Rick looked a bit more weak. He kept on about his grasshopper dreams all the time, and he kept crying, too. He seemed to cry a lot at that time.

I just wished he'd hurry up and get better. It made everybody miserable. Mummy went around looking all worried, and I had to be so quiet, and so careful what I said in case I said the wrong thing. Even Janie was different. I felt sorry for her, too. All the time Rick was ill she had even less appetite than ever. It really put her off her food.

Mummy and Janie thought in the end that the lumps on Rick's legs and arms were some kind of pimples. Well, they had to be. He kept saying they were bites, though, and he'd go on about his dreams again.

'Those grasshoppers are big, very big,' he said. 'And they've got big green fat bodies.' He began to shake, sort of, and held on to Janie's hand. Mummy said to Janie, 'I think we'll let him sleep in my room tonight,' and Janie said, 'Yes.'

Rick's bed was moved to Mummy's room that night, and he slept there. He seemed glad to be moving out of the nursery. I remember he smiled a bit as Janie carried him in her big, strong, country arms and laid him down between the soft sheets.

'You'll be all right now, my pet,' she whispered to him, and she kissed him softly on his forehead. I felt so sorry for poor Rick, so I sat with him until it was supper time. He was asleep when I left him.

It was strange being in the nursery alone, but I knew Janie was only a few yards away so I wasn't afraid.

When I went in to see Rick in the morning he looked much better. It was a great relief, Mummy said. And the day after that he looked better still. The pimples seemed to be going down a bit, they said, and that was a very good sign.

Mummy was especially glad because she had to go up to London to see her publishers or something, and she'd been worried about leaving him. She didn't need to, though – worry about him, I mean – not with Janie there.

Anyway, Rick got on so well that it wasn't long before he

was able to come downstairs. He couldn't run about yet – he still looked a bit pale – but he was so much better. It was at that time that we had a little party for his birthday. That was a lot of fun. We didn't play any moving-about games, but we played other games where you can sit down all the time, so it was all right. Rick looked happy then, and laughed, too. I remember I asked Janie to do some of her magic tricks, but she was too shy to do them with Mummy there. It's a shame because I know Mummy would have liked to see them.

The next day Mummy asked Rick if he'd be all right if she went away for a couple of days. He told her he would. She was glad about that and she phoned her publisher and said that she could get up to see him after all.

As London was a long way, Mummy was going to set off on the Monday and come back home on the Wednesday morning. It would just be the two nights that we'd be without her. 'Janie will look after you,' she said.

The night after Mummy had left for London, Rick slept in the nursery again. He wasn't afraid this time, though. It seemed that the grasshoppers, as he called them, didn't bother him anymore.

As a special treat, before we went to sleep, Janie did some more tricks for us. This time, instead of money, she used some of Rick's little toys – some of his tiny farm animals. He really laughed a lot. Mind you, she was clever. I wish Mummy could have seen it.

I don't know what time it was when I woke up, I just remember hearing a sort of scream coming from Rick's bed – or perhaps that was a part of my nightmare, too. It's all very mixed up, but I have a sort of picture of Rick sitting up in bed and brushing like crazy at his body. The room was all full of moonlight and I thought I saw, just for a second, a big fat shape kind of hop away. No, no, it didn't really hop, I don't think – it just looked as if it was *trying* to hop. I think I put on the light – I'm not sure – but it seemed very bright all of a sudden. Or maybe I was still asleep – yes, I think I was, because that's the time when I thought I saw it – this big fat grasshopper kind of thing. It was enormous, but the body wasn't green at all – not like Rick said. It was red – like the colour of blood. Then I was screaming as well. As I said, it's very mixed up, because then I can just remember Janie leaning over me – putting her arms around me, soothing me. The light was off and there was no sound at all from Rick's bed.

'You had a bad dream,' she whispered to me. Oh, I was so glad to hear her voice; I'd really been frightened for a minute. 'You probably ate too much cake,' she said. 'Go back to sleep now. Try to go to sleep.'

'I thought I saw – ' I started to shout a bit and she put up a finger to my lips.

'Ssshhhh. Don't speak so loud. You'll wake Rick.'

I looked over at Rick's bed and saw that he was sleeping very soundly. I whispered into Janie's ear, 'I was so scared. That's all the talk about *his* nightmares.' I was holding on to her hand very tight. 'Stay with me till I go back to sleep, will you?' I said.

'Of course, my pet. Of course I will, darling.'

The next day Rick had got his pimples back. He looked awful. Janie tried to get him to eat some breakfast, but he just shook his head. He looked so pale, poor thing, especially next to Janie's skin – her cheeks were so red.

He stayed in bed all day and he looked worse than I'd ever seen him before. I didn't have any nightmares at all that night, and I woke up feeling very good the next morning. That was until I looked over to Rick's bed. He wasn't in it, and all his sheets and blankets were tangled and pushed to one side.

Then I saw him.

My heart started bumping like mad and my stomach felt very funny. I think I screamed, sort of – anyway, I know I kept on saying his name:

'Rick! Rick! Oh, Rick . . . !'

See, he was lying on the little mat between our beds. His pyjamas were all twisted round – almost off – and I could see the little bumps all over his body. They were everywhere.

He'd probably scratched himself a lot, because I could see tiny smears of blood on his white skin.

I called out for Janie, then I jumped out of bed and knelt down by him. I put my arms around him. He was so cold. I started to talk to him like I'd heard Mummy and Janie talk to him: 'All right, my pet. All right, my darling. It's all right now. Caro's here.' He didn't look at me at all. His eyes were shut. He didn't move. I couldn't even feel him breathing. And still Janie didn't come. In the end I had to go and fetch her.

It was very hard to wake her. I had to keep on shaking her and shouting at the same time. When at last she woke and got up she looked all kind of heavy and puffy, the way some people do when they get up in the mornings.

I watched her as she looked at him, and I saw how her face went. Then she told me to put my dressing-gown on and go downstairs.

Rick was dead, you see. But I didn't know that until Janie told me later on. I'd never seen anyone dead before, and I remember wondering if they all looked that way.

All the days straight after that are very hazy. I've got all sorts of pictures in my mind. Things like Mummy standing in the front doorway, screaming and screaming, and later on crying all the time, and Janie trying to comfort her. There were doctors and other people coming to the house. They took Rick away somewhere. I can see myself wearing this black coat and standing next to my mother while they put this box into the ground. Rick was inside the box – I know it was true, but I could hardly believe it, because I thought about all those times when we played together. I loved my Rick even though he was a boy, yet now I can hardly remember what he looked like.

I can remember Janie, though. She was a real godsend then when my mother was crying all day long. Janie used to tell her not to cry. My mother would keep saying things like: 'Why? Why? Why?' Once I heard the doctor saying that Rick was a 'nemic', whatever that is. I probably haven't remembered everything properly – as I said – it all got very jumbled.

It seemed to be absolutely ages before things settled down again. Mummy was different somehow, but I started to do the things I used to do – like my games and things. It wasn't the same without Rick, though. It was a bit lonely without him. It felt as if there was something missing. Still, Janie was extra nice to me from then on, and she helped to make up for it. In the end I didn't think of him nearly as much.

I had the nursery to myself now, and Janie still slept in her own room with the door wide open, so I could always call her if I wanted to.

I started to have fun again. In a way I liked having Janie all to myself, too. When she did her tricks now she'd do them just for me.

'Do your tricks, Janie,' I'd say.

'And what will you give me if I do?' she'd say.

I used to say, 'Now, let me think.' and I'd offer her just about anything she wanted of all my toys. It was a kind of game we'd play, you see – but she used to say no to everything. Then I used to say: 'Well, Janie, the only thing I've got left is a kiss,' and she'd say, 'Well, that's just what I want,' or something like that. Then we used to laugh, and I'd kiss her, and then she'd do her tricks.

Oh, that Janie – you should have seen her. You should have seen the way she made those things happen! Pennies came out of her ears and her nose – they just seemed to fall out into her hand. Oh, I did love her so.

Everything seemed to be all right then. Except that later I think I caught what Rick had before he died.

I got up one morning and started scratching my leg. When I looked I saw this funny little lump there, like a big pimple, but not quite like a pimple. There was a tiny smear of blood there too. I told Mummy, and she seemed very worried.

The bumps got worse. The doctor came and looked at me a lot, but he just shook his head and I could tell that he didn't know what was the matter. I started to feel very funny – kind of weak. At the beginning I used to count the lumps, but in the end I had to stop; there were so many of them. Then Janie left and after that I got better.

I don't know why she left, but she did. Suddenly she just wasn't there one morning. I asked Mummy where Janie was, and Mummy told me that she'd gone and she wasn't coming back and that I'd better forget about her. She said to me, 'Janie's gone now, and you won't be seeing her again. You must put her right out of your head. Forget all about her.' I can remember Mummy's words so clearly because that whole night – Janie's last night – was funny in a way.

I had gone to sleep and I must have woken up again – scratching, or something. Anyway, I got up and went to Janie's room. I can remember stepping on some things on the carpet – funny-feeling things that felt – oh, funny under my bare feet. As I got to Janie's bed the moon came out all bright. I looked at Janie and then I went to get Mummy.

'Oh, what is it, darling?' Mummy said when I woke her up. I remember how sleepy she sounded. She put the light on and I pulled her hand.

'Come and see Janie, Mummy,' I said to her. 'She's so clever. She's so *funny*.'

Mummy said, 'Oh, go back to sleep, dear,' but I wanted her to come and I pulled her hand harder. She sat up then and started to get out of bed. 'Come on,' she said. 'You're going back to sleep. You're not well, young lady.'

'Yes, but you must look at Janie first,' I said. 'She's doing her tricks.'

'What do you mean, she's doing her tricks?' she said, but I just took her hand and pulled her along the landing into Janie's room. Mummy put on the light.

Oh, that Janie and her tricks! She was so clever! She couldn't stop doing her tricks even in her sleep. Even as we looked at her we saw this funny thing like a big grasshopper coming out of one ear. She kind of made it wriggle too. It was green and had a long, fat, funny-looking body. Then I saw a long feeler-like thing come out of one nostril, then a head followed it, then the body. One came out of the other nostril too. They were all over the place.

I remember I just stood there staring. Then Janie yawned – or pretended to yawn – and I saw this big green thing inside her mouth that poked its head over her lip and then came right out. Then my mummy started screaming and then, of course, Janie woke up.

Now it's all boring again.

CERA

*A*h, yes. Now the fire is taking hold, the flames are growing stronger. The sound of the ocean is quite drowned. When the flames are high enough and fierce enough I shall call the fire brigade. But not yet. Not till the fire's completely out of control. I can't take the chance of the firemen finding anything . . .

It's a shame about the beautiful house. Still, it matters little now. They won't be needing it any more. I wonder whether Greg ever did . . .

Greg Marchant and I grew up in the same little seaside town. But although we lived right next door to one another we never really became close friends. It was only later, after we had separated and gone our own ways, that our lives became inextricably involved. But while we were there, growing up to manhood side by side, we were apart. What was established between us was a quiet, reserved friendliness, one that was acknowledged, as it were, from the other side of a room.

One factor – and perhaps the main one – that inhibited any close relationship was the great difference in our respective heights. When fully grown I stood a solid six-foot-four in my bare feet, and Greg an unfortunate five-foot-one. I am sure that, for him as much as for me, the mere mental picture of us side by side was enough to stop us even from walking down the street together. The only times we ever felt at ease in one another's other's company, as I recall, were the few occasions when we happened to meet down on the beach where we swam. There, in the water, the disparity in our sizes didn't matter. Greg seemed more relaxed somehow, gaining a confidence which, on his own two feet, he seemed to lack.

He was a strange-looking young man – even without his

lack of stature. With his large, fleshy lips and small teeth, his ears flat to his head, he looked most unprepossessing. Once, when I remarked to my mother on his odd looks, and how different was his appearance from that of his parents, she told me that he had been adopted by the Marchants when he was just a baby. Where he had actually come from she did not know. Anyway, Greg was always there, quietly in the background. Until I left home to work in London – then he faded completely. And it was soon after that that I met Cera and fell so hopelessly in love with her.

Our meeting was, in a way, like some awful Hollywood film cliché. Whilst walking down Regent Street one spring afternoon she cannoned straight into me, catching me such a hefty clout on the cheekbone with her forehead that I was momentarily thrown off balance. We clutched each other for a second, like dancers caught in the midst of a step, then she, recovering her balance and her dignity, gave her apologies. She had some grit in her eye, she explained, blinking frantically, the tears streaming down her face, and it had momentarily blinded her. Of course, it was a heaven-sent opportunity for me and I lost no time in demonstrating my prowess with the corner of a handkerchief.

Her eyes were dark and round, rather small but enigmatic and quite captivating. I removed the offending foreign body and then, with my handkerchief, she dried her tears. In her hand I noticed that she held a pair of sunglasses.

'I had just taken them off to polish the lenses,' she said. 'Obviously I chose the wrong moment.'

She had a slight accent. It was almost as if her words were too carefully, too perfectly formed. I somehow had the feeling that perhaps she was Italian – perhaps she told me so – I can't remember.

I can remember how beautiful she was, though. Very beautiful. And tall. Almost as tall as I. Some men avoid very tall women – understandable in many cases – but I'm sure they wouldn't have avoided Cera . . . Cera . . .

'It's a beautiful name,' I told her. 'It suits you.' I spoke like some lovesick teenager. When she told me her last name I reacted with surprise. It was even more unusual.

'Tiidae,' I said. 'What kind of a name is that?'

She laughed in reply. 'Don't you like it? What can I do about it?'

'You could change it,' I said, laughing in return. 'You could change it to Robertson, for instance.'

'Your name wouldn't happen to be Robertson, would it?' she said.

I nodded gravely. 'You really are very astute.'

I made up my mind then that I wanted to marry her. And I think I might have been successful had not Greg Marchant come once more upon the scene.

Desperately in love, I invited her to spend the weekend at my parents' house by the sea. A village barbecue had been planned on the beach and I intended to make use of the festive atmosphere to help me in my proposal.

Everything was going well. With the villagers we sat around the fire on that warm, summer night, while the waves of the sea lapped gently just yards away. With the fading of the day Cera had taken off her dark glasses and now her bright eyes shone in the moonlight. She smiled at me, her lovely face framed by her thick, dark hair. I was deliriously happy. I watched her as she rose to her feet, standing above me tall and statuesque like a goddess of ancient times.

'I think, Carl, I would like to swim,' she said, looking down at me. 'Will you come?'

'In a moment,' I said. I wanted, for a while, the sheer pleasure of watching her from a distance; to bask in my proprietary glow.

She slipped the robe from her shoulders and stood there wearing a most becoming one-piece bathing suit. I could sense the eyes of the villagers turned towards her. Quite unaware, she smiled down at me. 'Don't be long, then.' With the words, she turned to move away.

She stopped so suddenly a moment later, that I looked at once to see what or who had attracted her attention.

It was Greg Marchant.

Rather amused at first, I looked from one to the other as they stood there some feet apart in the glow of the fire. Then I looked at Greg's face more closely. I'll never forget the look in his eyes as he gazed up at her from his lower vantage point. Yes, I remember thinking, you might well look at her so adoringly! But there's no chance for you, I'm afraid, my little friend!

When he came closer I got to my feet and made the necessary introductions. I fully expected that Cera would then make some polite excuse and continue to the water for her swim. But no, she stood there still, and suddenly, quite astounded, I saw the expression in her own dark brown eyes. Where I had expected to see amusement, tolerance, perhaps, I saw instead the reflection of Greg's own adoration! They stood there gazing at each other, rapt, as if no one else existed for them.

It was just my imagination, I told myself. Such a thing couldn't possibly be true! How could Greg Marchant, a mere five-foot-one, dream of ever making a match with Cera, who stood at least a foot taller? The idea was ludicrous! It was quite ridiculous.

But when I returned to London I came alone.

Two weeks later, still solitary in my flat, I read the newspaper clipping sent from home that told of the wedding of Mr Gregory Marchant and Miss Cera Tiidae. There was a wedding photograph, too. The top of his head came just to her shoulder.

'It's grotesque!' I said aloud. 'It can never work. The whole thing is just too silly.'

The smiles in the photograph were happy and I thought at once of their smiles and their laughter when I had watched them from the beach on the night of the barbecue. They had swum together, their bodies flashing, glinting in the moon-sparked water, their laughter bouncing back, echoing to the shore. I had felt embarrassed, but determined not to show it, the smile on my face growing more stiff and wooden with every second.

'Don't hate me, Carl,' Cera had pleaded an hour before I had left for my London train. 'I love him,' she had told me. 'Please try to understand.'

'*Understand!*' I had almost shouted the word back at her. How could she ask me to understand? How could she *expect* me to? She had known Greg for only two *days!* And in that time had thrown aside all that I had offered her. I would never understand, I told myself. Never. How could she do it to me? How? I was twenty-four years old and certain that I would never recover. I hated her then. I hated both of them. Desperately. Had she perhaps given me up for someone who was at least physically something of a challenge, it might have been easier to bear. But to lose out to someone who came to just above my elbow was a fact I just couldn't bear to think about.

But I *did* think about it. I couldn't stop thinking about it. The thought of Cera and Greg preyed on my mind till I was obsessed with them. I still couldn't believe that I had lost her. It was impossible, I kept telling myself. And yet, there it was. There, too, was the newspaper-clipping, the photograph, and the letter that had more recently arrived from Cera herself. In it she begged me once again to forgive and to try to understand. She was, she said, unbelievably happy. Greg was as well. And all their happiness, all their contentment, they owed to me. It was true; they did.

But they had destroyed *my* happiness, I thought. My own life was shattered. Well, in time they would pay. I was determined.

Another window in the lounge has just fallen out. Shivered in pieces. The heat must be building up in there. Still, it's not too hot to prevent my getting a quick look into the room. I can just make out the enormous shape there, smoke engulfed, lying on the carpet . . .

I thought so much about Cera and Greg that when, at last, we actually met – by chance – it came as no great surprise. I knew we would meet again sometime, somewhere.

On this occasion I was wandering aimlessly around the Natural History Museum in South Kensington. I had arrived there from the school nearby where I taught English and biology; having an engagement in the West End with a friend, it hardly seemed worthwhile going home to my flat in Wimbledon, so the museum was as good a place as any in which to kill an hour. The time was just after four-thirty. I had been amusing myself by gazing at a model of an angler fish. Quite inexplicably I had at once been reminded of Cera and Greg. The very size of the female compared with the male was enough to bring the pair at once into my thoughts again. I made my way to the cafeteria, bought a cup of coffee and a sandwich. And as I sat down I saw them, Greg and Cera, sitting at the table not far from mine. It was some moments before either of them saw me and I had, in those moments, ample opportunity to study them.

It must have been over five years since we had last met, I reckoned, and I only hoped that I had not changed quite so drastically in that time.

To be absolutely honest, I had never seen a more odd-looking couple in my entire life. Cera, I was sure, had grown larger than ever, while Greg, on the other hand, appeared to have shrunk. And it wasn't only in height that they had changed. They were different in bulk, also. Greg, moving past Cera to hand her a cup of tea or coffee, looked, I cruelly observed, like a satellite encircling the sun

What had I ever seen in her? I asked myself. She was, in a word, enormous.

And then they glanced round and saw me.

'Carl! Hallo!' Cera spoke first, her wide mouth smiling in surprise and gladness. Greg, close by her side, nodded, smiling an echo of her smile. He had lost a number of teeth, I noticed. At their insistence I joined them and together we talked for some minutes. I learned that they had bought a house very close to the sea – a large, very old house. No, Cera said, they had no children. I thought she spoke with a touch of sadness in her voice. She must have heard it herself, for she added quickly:

'We don't need children. We don't need anyone. We have each other.'

I found myself grinning and nodding like a marionette. The very thought of them being so close to each other, so content in each other's company, was somehow sickening to me; the smile was all I could manage.

When it was time for them to go they made me promise that I would visit them. Cera wrote out their address and gave it to me.

'Any time,' she insisted. 'We hardly ever go out ourselves. Please come.'

Again I nodded my agreement, having not the slightest intention of ever keeping to it. I watched as Greg got up and helped Cera to her feet. She moved slowly, shifting her enormous bulk without grace, looking like some huge, stranded sea creature. I was reminded again of the angler fish and her tiny mate as Greg moved around her, before her, and again in her wake, his movements quick and sharp, his eyes never wavering, never moving from the great bulk of his adored wife.

All the hatred I had harboured for so long was now, I discovered, mixed with an unbelievable feeling of disgust and revulsion. I felt it hit me, sweep over me like a wave.

For some moments after they had gone I sat quite still. My coffee cold and forgotten before me, my sandwich drying on its plate. After a while I got up and, as if in a daze, moved away. My footsteps, I found, were leading me back to the Fish Gallery.

The whole room is ablaze now. No one could possibly get to them . . .

I did visit them eventually. At the time I told myself that it was because I was in the vicinity of Thorsall Down. But that's not really true. I know it now. I wanted to see them. I had to.

Ever since the day in the Natural History Museum I had found myself devoured by a desire to see them again ... Cera and Greg ... those repulsive objects of my growing hatred.

I found the house without difficulty. It stood high up on the cliff overlooking the sea. The only approach to the front door was by means of a narrow pathway that wound through a wild, tangled garden, formless and unkempt. The hard, late November winds had all but stripped the trees of their last leaves, and as I stepped from my car I wondered how anyone could find pleasure in such a bleak, forbidding atmosphere.

With my collar pulled up high about my ears I made my way along the path to the old porch. My ring at the bell was answered by an old woman who took my name and then retreated quickly into the shadows. Moments later she was back and ushering me into a large, warm room. Giving me a nod and a rather uncertain smile, she left me. And then Cera and Greg appeared.

The light in the room was quite dim but I could see well enough that in the six months since our last meeting the couple had changed even more.

I found myself wondering whether the drastic changes would have taken place had they never met each other. If Cera had married me would she still have become this gross, obscene creature that I now saw before me? Would Greg, left to his life in his hometown, still have developed into this little toothless, quick-moving caricature of a man?

Cutting into my thoughts came Cera's precise accents as she asked if I would stay for dinner. Taken by surprise, I heard myself accept her invitation, cursing inwardly a second later, for there was nothing I wanted more than to say my hurried goodbyes and go.

I eventually left after about two hours. They had to be the longest two hours of my life.

For what seemed ages after the front door closed behind me I remember standing at the end of the long garden path breathing in the clear autumn air in great gulps. Clutching the handle of my car door I fought against the nausea that arose in me. My eyes clenched as tightly as my fists, I tried to dispel the images that swam in my mind, threatening to swamp me. But the pictures wouldn't go. I watched all over again as Greg sat at the table – so close to Cera that their bodies often touched – eating from a bowl a mess of soggy, sloppy pap that she had served him.

'Poor darling cannot chew since he lost all his teeth,' she explained with loving sympathy in her voice.

She and I ate some dish of meat and vegetables. I ate without tasting a mouthful, so desperately eager was I to get away. But for the moment there was no escape. I was forced to watch as Cera picked up a spoonful of the slop from Greg's dish and fed him, gently pushing the bowl of the wooden spoon between his thick, fleshy lips, past his pink, toothless gums. He slobbered, nestling into her gigantic bosom, the food dribbling down over his weak chin as if he no longer had complete control over himself. And Cera didn't seem bothered in the least; she appeared to be as fond, as adoring of him as ever. The spectacle was sickening.

Later, as I headed back to London, I said to myself that two such hideous people should not be allowed to go on living.

I had to do it. I had no choice. I only hope that no one will ever know. I pray it. But the fire must make sure of it ... The fire. Nothing can be seen inside the room now ... only the flames ... The flames are everywhere ...

Of course I went back again. I had sworn to myself that I never would but of course I did. I knew I would have to. It was March when I retraced my steps along the narrow, winding garden path. As before, I had made no announcement of my impending arrival and I thought, just for a moment, that they had gone away; I could see no lights shining through the curtains. It was with some relief that I heard the footsteps coming to answer my ring at the door. In another two minutes I was being shown into the lounge by the old servant I had seen previously. When she had gone I sat down, waiting patiently for Cera and Greg to come in and greet me.

The room was large and lit only by the firelight and one small lamp. Outside, a wind had sprung up, buffeting the house in its exposed position, crying round the corners. Its sound made a forlorn, melancholy background to the bright crackle of the burning log in the grate. And then came the sound of Cera's voice.

'It's so nice to see you, Carl. And such a surprise. Come and sit over here by me.'

Having turned in the direction of her voice I at last made out her shape as she lounged in the shadows.

'Hallo, Cera . . .'

I moved to her and sat in the chair which she indicated. Before me her huge bulk was draped over a red velvet couch, the legs of which must surely have been groaning beneath her weight. I studied her in the fitful glow of the fire.

There was no longer even the remotest trace of the girl I had met in Regent Street all those empty, unhappy years ago. She bore hardly any likeness to a woman at all now, and I shuddered to imagine what she must look like divested of her clothing. Her shape was not smooth as one might have expected, but oddly lumpy, and the flickering firelight playing on the great mound of her body gave, I thought, beneath the folds of her loose robe, the strange impression of movement.

I looked at her face. Her mouth with its strong, sharp, white teeth looked wider than before, while her little round eyes, set in the increasing expanse of her pale flesh, seemed almost to have disappeared. I looked away again.

'Where is Greg?' I asked.

For a long moment she hesitated, then she said:

'He is away.' A pause, then she added: 'It is a pity you cannot see him. He will be sorry to have missed you.'

I was about to ask more specifically where he was when she forestalled me with a question of her own.

'Did you come by train?'

'No. By car again. I parked it on the road like last time. I could find no garage or any other suitable spot.'

'There is none.' She shook her head and her whole body seemed to quiver.

'Then where do you keep your car?'

'We have no need of a car,' she answered. 'We have no need to go anywhere. Everything we need is here. Whatever provisions we require are brought to the house. And we have our servants. We manage very well.' After a pause, she added – with, I thought, a trace of smugness – 'We are very self-sufficient here.'

At this point the maid came to the door and announced that if nothing more was wanted then she and the cook would like to leave for the night.

'Thank you, dear.' Cera smiled. 'We'll see you in the morning.'

When the maid had gone, Cera said with a shrug, 'It is impossible to get servants to live in . . .'

'It must be expensive, running a large house like this,' I said, ' – servants as well.'

'Oh, well – ' another smile came, showing her white teeth, 'as I said before, we manage.'

I realised suddenly how very little I knew about her. What was her background? Obviously she had considerable wealth; neither she nor Greg seemed to have done a stroke of work since their marriage.

'Are you surprised to see me?' I asked.

'No.' She shook her head. 'I thought you would come again.'

'Are you sorry I came?'

She looked away from me. She spoke softly.

'Perhaps it would be better if you did not come back . . .'

'Yes . . .' She was right. In a moment, I determined, I would get up, go, and never come back. What was I doing here now? I asked myself. It was insane. I rose to my feet and picked up my coat. 'No, please,' I said, gesturing as she began to move her great bulk off the couch. 'I can see myself out.'

'Nonsense. We don't forget our manners. We'll see you to the door.'

As she got to her feet I could see at last just how enormous she had become. She must be pregnant, I thought – unless she was very ill . . . But it was not her weight alone. Surely she was now taller than I. The level of her small, button-like eyes was higher than my own. Looking down, I tried to see whether she was wearing high-heels, but the length of her robe hid her feet from view. I became aware once more that beneath her robe there was some flickering of life, a pulsating that must be, I told myself, a trick of the light.

'Goodbye, Cera . . .'

'Goodbye, Carl. Perhaps someday you will understand.'

Never, I said to myself.

'Well . . .' Cera out her hand and, hesitating for the briefest moment, I took it. The feel of her flesh was cool and clammy. Quickly I released her and, much relieved, moved to the door. Behind me she followed, moving slumberously, tortuously, her great, unwieldy body swaying with her slow, graceless steps. And then the door was opening and I was out into the air again, hurrying away down the path back to normality. I could feel Cera's eyes upon me as I went. As I reached a corner I turned and looked back; she was still there, framed in the soft light of the doorway, looking like a monstrous, grotesque museum specimen.

My sleep that night was fitful. I awoke many times, and each time, it seemed, Cera's body was there before me; and then Greg, small and insignificant in the shadow of her overpowering bulk. And even in my dreams she was there, swimming by, floating by, the folds of her loose, voluminous robes drifting, undulating, twitching around her. In the morning I got up thick-headed, and unsteady on my feet from lack of sleep.

I went through my day at school with my mind only half

on my job. And all the while my thoughts of Cera and Greg were lurking there, ready to take over. I grew more and more obsessed with them with every passing hour.

I put my obsession down to the fact that, quite simply, they needed *explaining*. It was just that. They were beyond my understanding, and I couldn't let such a mystery rest. Had they always been quite so grotesque, always so repellent? Was the change in them existing only in my own imagination? There were so many questions.

When I got back to my flat later that afternoon I at once searched for the newspaper clippings that I had kept for so long. I smoothed at the yellowing photograph and looked at the smiling faces there. They looked young and happy. Cera's smile was dazzling, and there below was Greg's grinning face as she towered above him like some giant protectress.

I turned to the newsprint and read again the words that had, at one time, so devastated my own happiness: '. . . at the marriage of Mr Gregory Marchant and his bride, the former Miss Cera Tiidae . . .'

'Tiidae . . .' I said the name aloud. And I recalled my own words when she had first told me her name: 'What kind of a name is that?' I had asked jokingly. Cera . . . Tiidae . . . Cera Tiidae. In my mind the names rolled around, moving, shifting . . . It was almost as if my brain wanted only the merest jolt for the pieces to fall into place . . . Cera . . . Tiidae . . . It meant something to me – if only I could find what it was.

Casting my mind back I searched my experiences for a clue. There was something there – I knew it – something that would give my mind the necessary jolt. It was something connected with one of our meetings . . . The beach . . . No . . . Where else had we met? At their house in Thorsall Down and in the cafeteria of the museum.

Click. It was the proverbial piece of puzzle falling into place.

If I was right.

No. *No!* I must be mistaken, I told myself. I must be wrong!

The whole idea, the whole conception, was too dreadful to contemplate.

When the Natural History Museum opened this morning I was waiting on the steps. I had already telephoned the head-master of my school to say that I might be a little late. Now, hurrying past the surprised doormen, I went at once to the gallery where the fish exhibits were kept. There, striding pur-posefully between the rows of glass cases, I came at last to the end where the model of the angler fish was kept.

My heart pounding, I stared at the grotesque creatures. There was the enormous female with the wide mouth and the tiny button-like eyes. And there was the male, so small beside in comparison. And there was the name: *Ceratias holboelli (family: Ceratiidae)* . . . *Ceratiidae* . . . Cera Tiidae . . .

But how could it be? How was it possible? That was some-thing I would never know, I was certain. I was only sure that it was so . . . I found myself holding on to the sides of the case for support. My head was so low that my breath was misting the glass. I shook myself and stood straight. I must be living in some terrible nightmare. Soon I would awaken, relieved beyond measure to have escaped such awful reality. But I knew it was no dream. Trembling slightly, I went on to read the rest of the neatly-printed information. It explained many things: the absence of Greg, the strange movements beneath her robe, her grossness, and slowness of gait.

In the men's lavatory a few minutes later I was violently sick. Afterwards I phoned the school again, this time to tell them I would not be in. Then, with my new-found knowledge, I drove back to Wimbledon where I sat in my kitchen for long hours over numerous cigarettes and cups of coffee. Very late in the afternoon I came to a decision. I would go back. Quickly I got into my car and drove away.

It was quite dark when at last I parked my car and walked up the garden path. The servants would have left by now, I thought. I was glad of that. Ahead of me the large house was, as before, quite quiet. I rang the bell and waited. I rang again.

After ten minutes of ringing and waiting it was obvious to me that there would be no answer. I tried the door, found it opened to my touch, and went in.

Entering the lounge I found a bright fire burning in the hearth; the top log had only just caught, so it was clear that the room had very recently been vacated.

'Cera . . . ?'

I waited, listening, but there was no reply to my call. The French windows leading to the cliff-top were wide open. I crossed the room and stood, breathing in the salt, night air. Below me the sea stretched away into the distance, dark, mysterious, hiding who-knew-what unbelievable, unfathomable secrets.

Moving quickly down the shallow steps I went out on to the hard, rocky surface and looked down. The moon had risen, its light sparking off the waves as they broke over the stones at the foot of the cliff.

For some minutes I remained there, peering out across the water, my eyes straining in the light. And then, with a start, I saw them.

Frantically, nervously, I searched about me till I had located the head of a narrow path leading to the beach below. Hurrying, and careless of my safety, I scrambled down, almost falling in my anxiety to reach the bottom.

At the water's lapping edge I stood, watching and waiting. Nearby on a large rock was draped her robe; I knew she would soon come to shore.

And there she was. Suddenly. Just thirty yards away, her head breaking the waves in the path of the moon's reflection. As yet she had not caught sight of me. I knew it would be just a matter of seconds before she did, though, and I prayed that first of all I would have a chance to see. I had to know. For certain. The next moment I did.

As I watched, holding my breath, she found her footing

in the sand and heaved her huge body out of the water. And for one brief, dazzlingly-clear instant I saw them. In the same second she saw me.

'Carl!'

My name issuing from her lips was nearly a scream. It was followed almost at once by a loud splash as she threw herself back into the sea, taking cover beneath its darkened surface. I did not move.

'Carl . . . ?'

Looking over to my right I saw her head above the waves.

'Yes . . . ?'

'Please,' she said, ' – close your eyes. Just for a moment.'

With my eyes tight shut I waited. Her voice came again, closer at hand now.

'All right.'

I saw that she was standing about five yards away from me. We faced each other across the sand. The robe that had lain on the rock was now clutched tightly to her body.

'Thank you,' she said quietly.

'It doesn't matter,' I said. 'I saw.'

'Yes.' She nodded and turned her head away from me. 'I didn't want you to. I had hoped – we had hoped – that no one would ever know.'

'It suddenly came to me,' I said. 'Quite by chance. The idea. Then I made it my business to find out. For certain. I had to.'

'And what will you do – now that you know?' She was staring at me intently.

'I hated you,' I said. 'Both of you. I wanted so desperately to hurt you. As I had been hurt.'

'That was a long time ago.'

'Yes. But some injuries take longer to heal.' I paused briefly, then, my voice even, I added:

'You disgust me.'

She flinched slightly as if I had struck her. Her body shook. Moments of silence went by, and she repeated her question:

'What are you going to do, Carl?'

Suddenly, she was crying. Tears spilled from her small, round eyes and trickled down her wide, fleshy cheeks. I wished I had never come. If only I could have been content with not knowing ... But it was too late for that. Turning quickly I strode back in the direction of the cliff path. Behind me her voice cried out in sudden anguish.

'Carl! Wait!'

I walked on.

'Carl! Please! What are you going to do?'

I wouldn't listen. Mentally shutting my ears to the sound I hurried over the sand. Reaching the path, I began to clamber up. Behind me the sound of her sobs punctuated her laboured breathing as she strove to catch up. Looking over my shoulder I saw her as, clutching her body, she stumbled along in my wake, her voice, hollow with fear, crying out again and again.

I was half-way up the cliff path when I heard her pleadings turn to a scream of terror and pain. I spun. Looking down I saw her where she had fallen, lying sprawled out in the moonlight. In seconds I was at her side.

'Are you all right?' I knelt in the sand, anxiously watching the pain fleeting in spasms across her face.

'I think so.' She spoke as if with effort.

'Both of you?'

'I think so.' She stiffened for a split-second, grimacing as a sudden stab of pain caught at her breath. With her hands and arms she hugged her body, protective, comforting. 'Help me, please,' she said.

Steadying her enormous weight as best I could, I helped her to her feet. How we made it to the top of the cliff I shall never know. But somehow we managed it. Panting, gasping for breath I helped her up the steps and in through the French windows. There, as if every ounce of her strength had been used, she collapsed, falling on the floor in a heap.

'Cera ... Cera ...' I was by her again, reaching out to her, touching her cold, clammy skin. 'I'm sorry,' I murmured. 'I'm sorry.'

'It doesn't matter now.' She tried to smile at me but somehow the smile didn't quite work. 'It'll be all right,' she said. Her robe had fallen open when she fell, and in the flickering glow from the fire I could see clearly the small body of her mate. His arms and legs wrapped around her, he clung there, his head just above the level of her great pendulous breasts. I remembered what I had read in the museum. I knew that, if I looked more closely, I would see that his mouth had joined itself to her flesh, the skin of his large lips fusing with her skin, his blood supply coming directly from her own. No longer having any life of his own, Greg had become completely parasitic, depending upon his mate for the gift of life itself. I wondered why it is that parasites should appear so physically loathsome? Greg was no exception. Bearing absolutely no resemblance to any human form he held on to his saviour, his lover, his wife. He looked like nothing so much as some grotesque, monstrous, cancerous growth.

'Carl ...' Cera had seen the expression in my eyes. 'Don't look like that,' she said softly. 'We are what we are.'

'I'm sorry.'

'Cover us, please ...'

I wrapped the robe around her, around them both. It wasn't the warmth that she was seeking, I thought, but privacy from my shocked, commenting gaze. After a moment she said:

'I am hurt, Carl ... The fall ...' She winced as a stab of agony underlined her words and a little bubble of blood formed from the corner of her mouth, became a trickle and ran down to disappear beneath the collar of her robe.

'I could get a doctor,' I suggested, knowing that the idea was ridiculous. She shook her head.

'No. No doctor. There are some things that should always be secret.'

And then she was turning, trying to lie on her side, the blood gushing out of her mouth and her nose, her small, fish-like eyes rolling in her head. Underneath the fabric of her robe

I was aware of a sudden movement. It was Greg, beginning his own futile fight for survival. It wouldn't last long, I knew.

I knelt at Cera's side, quite helpless in the face of her desperation. How she fought! How she struggled to cling to her unlovely existence.

But at last it was over.

For some moments after Cera died Greg continued with his small, jerky movements, till in the end they faded away and grew still. I rose to my feet, my knees stiff from the period of kneeling. Below me in a pool of blood lay Cera's body, her arms still shielding the degenerate form of her mate as, clutched to her still breast, he lay upon her.

I couldn't leave them like that, I decided, and recalled her words that some things are best left secret. It is true. Particularly such a secret as hers. It was as I lit a cigarette with an ember from the fire that the thought came to me. I debated only for seconds before making my decision. It is final . . .

The curtains caught so easily, the flames running straight up to lick at the low-beamed ceiling. It won't take long at all, I thought . . .

There is no one about. In this desolate spot it seems that more than a fire is needed to attract attention. But someone will be along sooner or later. Perhaps I won't bother to telephone the fire brigade after all. What can they do? Nothing. It would serve no purpose. Anything that mattered was beyond all control a long, long time ago . . .

ONE OF THE FAMILY

GUY ALLENBURY ran along the path. Behind him, and coming dangerously close, came the ferocious snarling of the dog as it scrabbled from the house in angry pursuit. But there ahead was the gateway. In the nick of time Guy leapt through, slamming the gate shut in the face of his would-be attacker. Distantly from the house the shouting and cursing could still be heard. Closer, and separated only by the high gate, the dog continued to growl.

Through a gap between the gate boards Guy peered at the dog, an ugly brute of some indeterminate breed, grossly overfed and overweight. Its angry growls punctuated by the most disgusting snuffling sounds, it threw itself at the barrier in an effort to get out. Not the most prepossessing specimen, Guy observed, noting the single ear and the large areas of bald white flesh amid the stubbly dull brown hair. 'Certainly,' he said aloud, 'I've had more attractive pursuers.'

As he stood there in the narrow street, panting, trying to get his breath back, he thought of his mother's words to him before he had left:

'You let me hear how you get on, darling. Tell me what kind of reception you get. I just know you're going to have a *wonderful* time.' He grinned now at the memory, shaking his head. Oh, yes, he would tell her. 'My Uncle Joe and his wife,' he would say when next he wrote, 'didn't exactly put out the welcome mat.' And no, indeed they hadn't, he said to himself, but they were the exception, surely – the others would be okay.

With a last look back at the house he moved to the kerb, swung a long leg astride his hired bicycle and pushed off.

Leaving the small town behind him, he cycled deeper into the countryside, heading in the general direction of Harkinbridge, the small village that was next on his list. He sang as he rode, the rhythm of his feet eating up the miles that sped beneath his spinning wheels. When he reached the top of the next hill, he promised himself, he would stop for a rest, have a little light refreshment, and take another look at his list.

Five minutes later he had wheeled his bicycle onto the grass verge beside the road, and sat down. From his backpack he took a flask of hot coffee and a packet of ham sandwiches. And he relaxed, leaning back and stretching his legs. Leisurely he ate and drank, enjoying the taste, enjoying the warmth and the freshness of his first English summer.

Twenty-four years old, Guy was on vacation from his home in New York City and was spending this particular week on a cycling tour of the West Country. His sojourn, though, was not merely for the purpose of seeing the homeland of his father and mother; he was also intent on contacting any of his relatives who might live in the area. From the information gathered from his parents, he had made up a list.

Brushing the crumbs from his shirt front, he took the list from his pocket. Pursing his lips, he read the names.

So far, he hadn't met with much success. Of the fourteen people named on the paper three had moved to addresses that were unknown to the present house-occupiers, and where they were now was anybody's guess. A further six had been traced to spots from which they would never move, spots marked by gravestones that were fast disappearing beneath the encroachment of unchecked cemetery weeds.

With four of the others he had got some measure of satisfaction – if satisfaction was the right word. At least, he comforted himself, he had been able to make some kind of contact with them. Though now, looking back, he wasn't at all sure that he wouldn't rather have missed the pleasure of those meetings.

The first one had been with Beryl – his cousin on his father's side – and her husband Bill. It was the latter who had answered Guy's knock. Bill had stood there in the open doorway, grinning widely, showing numerous gaps in a row of buck teeth. When Guy explained who he was, and why he was there, the stranger had gaped at him for a second then, turning, had called loudly up the narrow stairs.

'Beryl . . . Beryl . . .' he yelled, 'there's somebody 'ere to see you.' He winked conspiratorially at Guy, and added, yelling, 'Says he's your cousin. And a foreigner by the sound of 'im.'

A moment later Beryl had appeared.

Guy saw first her legs as she came clumping down the stairs; big, heavy legs clad in thick dark stockings, her feet encased in an enormous pair of carpet slippers that at once brought to mind memories of ferry boats on the Hudson River. Then at the door she stopped, facing him, a tall, solid-looking young woman with a smile as dazzling as her husband's, her piercing blue eyes permanently at odds with each other in the most unbelievable squint.

'My cousin,' Beryl cried when once more Guy had stated his business. 'Our uncle Arthur's son! Fancy that now!' Her words came in a thick, almost unintelligible accent. 'And all the way from America, too.'

Throwing her arms around him, she gave him a loud, wet, smacking kiss full on the mouth. The next second she was dragging him inside the house and thrusting him into a large, lumpy armchair by the fireplace.

'Oh, what a surprise!' she said. 'What a nice surprise! Ain't this a nice surprise, Bill!'

'Oh, ah!' Bill nodded emphatically, winking at Guy with his gap-toothed smile. 'Oh, ah – it certainly is!'

'Well, now . . .' Beryl sat in the chair opposite Guy, her hands clasped before her in rapturous delight. 'Tell me. I want to hear *all* about you! *Everything!* And all about what you're doin' over 'ere in this part of the world. Put the kettle on, will you, lovie?'

Guy was rather taken by surprise by the last request, then realised that it was directed at her husband. Since Beryl was able to look at both men at the same time – even though they sat some distance apart – it tended to become rather confusing. With some relief Guy watched as Bill got up from his seat in the window and hurried out to the kitchen. 'Yes, we'll 'ave a nice cup o' tea, Guy,' Beryl said. 'That'll be nice. Won't that be nice, eh?'

Guy nodded dumbly. He had heard legends of English hospitality, but, somehow, about to experience it first-hand, he quailed slightly. A little moment of silence went by, and then Beryl said,

'Well, come on, then. Tell us what you're doin' round 'ere, then.'

Guy took a breath and began, but no sooner did he mention the main object of his tour when, without a second's hesitation, Beryl launched into a full account of the comings and goings of the Allenbury family. Once started, it was as if she would never stop.

An hour later she was still going strong with no sign whatever of flagging.

'. . . And then, of course, there was Aunt Emily.' Her voice droned on. 'She's the one what married Bob Chandler. Didn't last, though – the marriage. Well, we knew it wouldn't. Went off with the milkman in the end . . .'

'Oh, really?' Guy was bored to distraction.

'Yes, quite a shock, I can tell you. But to Emily most of all. I mean, fancy Bob going and doing a thing like that. It wouldn't have been so bad but the milkman didn't have no class. No class at all. But there,' she sighed, 'there's no accounting for taste.'

'No, I guess not.' Guy shifted uncomfortably in his chair; his buttocks were numb. Very slightly he raised himself up, hoping the blood would flow back unimpeded, bringing the return of feeling, a little life. His efforts were in vain.

'. . . And then of course there was Bert,' Beryl went on, ' – the one what married Cousin Lucy, the one what had the twins, who we don't talk about. One of 'em went off to the Arctic, or one of them places, while the other got mixed up with some slut of a barmaid who was married to this climber who invited Ronnie out one day and shot 'im up the mountain. Terrible business . . .'

And so it went on. And on. Through tea, through scones with butter and honey. Through more tea. Eyes glazed, pupils dilated, Guy sat there, trying unobserved to massage feeling back into his cramped limbs. At last he could bear it no longer and, fixing Beryl's squint with his most determined expression, he got shakily to his feet.

'Well, it's been really kind of you,' he said, 'but I think I ought to be moving on,' and took a step forward. Unfortunately his right leg had gone to sleep and he was only just able to prevent himself from falling headlong. Recovering, he stumbled to the door, as he did so giving a little laugh, rather forced, but hoping to show nonchalance, light-hearted acknowledgment of his uncoordinated gait.

'Oh, nonsense!' With her words, Cousin Beryl grabbed him in her strong arms, so suddenly that he was thrown once more off balance. With a muffled murmur of protest he fell against her huge bulk. 'You can't go yet,' Beryl said. 'We're goin' to have some more tea.' She motioned to Bill. 'Put the kettle back on, lovie.'

Guy fought to regain his breath and his footing. 'No, no, really. I must go,' he protested. 'It's been really great and I hate to leave, but I must.' He shrugged and gave his laugh again. 'You know how it is. Ha ha.'

'But I haven't told you about Aunt Lavinia yet,' Beryl said, reaching out for him again. 'She was the one what went on the streets and –'

'Next time. Tell me all about it next time.' Guy sounded almost incoherent in his desperation as he dodged the big red clutching hands. 'It'll have to be next time, I'm afraid.' And then he was grabbing his pack, pulling it on and edging through the doorway. 'Do excuse me, please.' Backing out now and down the steps. 'I'll tell Mom I met you. She'll be real thrilled, I know.' There was the front gate, his bicycle . . . 'I'll call again soon. Real soon.' And he was moving off, waving in the early evening light. 'Goodbye . . .'

As he disappeared around the bend in the road Beryl turned to Bill.

'Well,' she sniffed, miffed, 'if that's the way them Yanks go on then they can stay in America. Best place for 'em.' She led the way back into the house and sat down, one eye fixed on her smiling husband, and the other on some unremarkable spot on the ceiling. 'Some people just don't know 'ow to behave, that's their trouble.' She sighed again, deeply. 'Well, what can you expect? He's from America. If you ask me it's just as well we gave the place up.'

Pedalling madly along the country lanes, Guy concentrated on putting the maximum distance between himself and Cousin Beryl. Just my luck, he thought, to land with somebody like that. Still, the others would be all right. After all, he said to himself, every tree must have a couple of unsound fruit. He would put Cousin Beryl from his mind, he decided, and think about the next one.

The next one – of those living – turned out to be a very ancient, doddering grandmother – his maternal grandmother, a Lampton.

At the door of her tiny house he towered above her, repeating, 'I'm your grandson,' in successively louder tones, trying to penetrate her deafness. The hearing-aid she wore seemed to have little effect. Until she switched it on.

'So you're my grandson!' she said. 'You don't sound like you comes from round these parts . . .'

'No,' Guy said. 'I'm Ellen's son.'

'Ellen? Ellen who?'

'Ellen Lampton . . . *Your* Ellen . . .' Then rather lamely he added, 'Your daughter?' Really, he thought, such elucidation shouldn't be necessary. He was beginning to doubt his own knowledge.

'Oh, *that* Ellen,' said Grandma. 'You mean the one that

went off to America. Why didn't you say so?' She reached out a bony hand. 'Well, come on in.'

Minutes later, sitting in her little warm kitchen with the flies buzzing around his head, he watched her as she rocked back and forth in her old rocking chair. At her insistence he told her – in a loud voice – of his mother and father in New York. All the while she nodded away at him, her wet, near-toothless gums smacking in the most off-putting manner. It was worse than Beryl's squint, he thought. But he persevered, in spite of her constant fidgeting, in spite of her interruption when she broke in to ask him – very sweetly:

'Who did you say you are?'

Gradually, though, she became more attentive, her rocking ceased and he began to feel that the afternoon wouldn't be such a complete write-off after all. At last he rose to go, moved to her and leaned down close to her ear.

'Well, goodbye, Grandma.' He supposed he ought to at least kiss her before he left.

'Grandma . . . ?'

A loud, rasping snore greeted his gentle word. For Christ's sake, he murmured as he let himself out, and there he'd thought she was hanging on every goddamn word. He nodded back at the sleeping woman. 'I'll tell Mom you send your love . . .'

And so onward – or downward – through the list. Next was Uncle Maurice.

Uncle Maurice Lampton – mother's half-brother – promised to be quite different.

Guy found his name in the telephone directory, dialled the number and was at once invited round for dinner that very evening.

Uncle Maurice, it turned out, lived alone in a large, rambling, simply furnished house on the outskirts of the village of Marshleigh. He was, by all accounts, a most successful novelist. Guy had never actually read any of his works, and couldn't recall seeing the name Maurice Lampton on any book cover

– still, he promised himself, he would catch up on his uncle's literary creations just as soon as he was able. For the moment it was enough that they would meet. It was exciting to have a famous novelist in the family, Guy thought; and, thank God, at last he might encounter a little civility, intelligence and polish.

From the moment when he first saw Uncle Maurice, Guy knew he was going to like him. And his first impressions were never wrong. Standing well over six feet and correspondingly broad, Maurice looked tough, strong, and considerably younger than his fifty-two years. His handshake was firm, and the friendly slap on the back he gave Guy made him stagger.

Wonder of wonders, in addition to everything else, Maurice turned out to be a marvellous cook. The variety of courses he served were a delight from start to finish. In short it was a wonderful meal, the conversation was bright and interesting, and flowed as generously as the wine. Now, at last, Guy told himself, he'd be able to write home something positive about one of his relatives. Praise the Lord.

The evening was turning out to be such a success that when Guy was invited to stay overnight he readily accepted.

'You'll be much better off here,' Uncle Maurice said, 'than in that stuffy little hotel.'

'I'm sure I will.' Guy nodded in agreement, his head slightly muzzy from the wine. 'But I don't want to put you to any trouble.'

'It's no trouble at all,' Maurice assured him. 'Think nothing of it.'

Over coffee Guy asked Uncle Maurice about his writings.

With a flourish, Maurice reached up and took from a shelf some books which, proudly, he displayed in a long, colourful line. He wrote, so it appeared going by the jacket designs, novels about beautiful young heroines who became trapped in desperate situations in remote, towering mansions on the edges of cliffs. Each of the covers Guy saw depicted a young heroine fleeing in terror from some desperate situation. Invariably she was shown running – usually through overgrown grass – with her hands clutching at the skirts of her long dress. In each background an enormous house rose up through the mist. Guy wondered why he had not come across any of these impressive-looking buildings; if Uncle Maurice's books were anything to go by, such houses must be all over the place.

In spite of a slight sense of disappointment over the nature of Uncle Maurice's literary matter, Guy tried to make the right noises of approval. Even so, the name on each lurid jacket did give him some pause for thought.

'It says here,' he said, 'by Louisa Clements.'

'Yes, that's right,' said Maurice. 'That's me.'

Guy's heart sank a little more, then, Oh, what the hell, he thought – hundreds of writers do it. So what was so odd about a little pseudonym?

'Let me show you around,' Uncle Maurice was saying. 'That's if you'd like to, of course.'

'Of course,' said Guy, readily. 'I'd love to.' He rose from his chair.

Carefully, lovingly, Uncle Maurice gathered up Louisa Clements' masterpieces and replaced them reverently upon the shelf. He turned, smiling, and beckoned Guy to follow him.

Walking behind his host up the wide staircase, Guy observed two large white cats that passed him on their way down, moving lithely from step to step. 'Alice and Maureen,' Uncle Maurice remarked.

On the landing were three more cats: Crystal, Lottie and Theda. And in Uncle Maurice's room two more: Margaret and Edgar.

'Just one male among so many females,' Guy said. 'He must have a terrific time.'

'Oh, no.' Maurice shook his head. 'He's been taken care of. We can't have that sort of thing going on.'

Guy gave the cat a brief look of condolence before following his uncle from the scarlet-draped bedroom. 'I'll show you your room before we go any further,' Uncle said, and stopped outside a small door at the end of the landing. Opening the door, he gestured for Guy to enter. Guy stepped forward, then stopped in the open doorway, gazing into the room. At his side, Uncle Maurice gave him a slightly anxious smile. 'You'll be quite comfortable, I'm sure,' he said. Then after a pause added, 'It's more comfortable than it looks, you know.'

'I'm sure it is . . .' Guy swallowed, at a loss for words. Around his feet the cats moved, silky, smooth, insinuating, rubbing against his legs. Guy sneezed. Then again. And again.

'Oh, I hope you're not catching a cold,' said Uncle Maurice, patting Guy's shoulder.

'I forgot to mention,' said Guy, sneezing again, 'that I'm allergic to cats. I don't think I shall be able to stay after all. What a shame.'

It wasn't only the cats, though. It wasn't only the sight of the black-draped bed surrounded by the black candles. It wasn't only Uncle Maurice's strong, hairy hand resting intimately on his shoulder; no, most of all it was the formidable array of strange items that hung on the black walls: the whips, the ropes, the chains, the handcuffs, the thumb-screws, and the numerous other odd-looking gadgets whose uses Guy could only guess at. He forced another series of sneezes.

'It's no use,' he gasped, trying desperately to make his eyes water. 'I'll have to go. It'll just keep on all night otherwise.'

'But you were all right when you came in,' Uncle Maurice said. 'It came on so suddenly. Perhaps if you wait a bit it'll go away.'

Guy shook his head. 'I don't think it will.' He added a sad note to his voice, moved back out to the landing. 'I don't think it will at all . . .'

His next meeting had been the briefest of all. This was with Cousin Joe Allenbury and his wife, Morffyd, a mean-looking, pinched-up little Welsh woman.

Joe had opened the door to Guy and really appeared most pleased to see him. Everything, thought Guy, was going to be fine. That was until Morffyd came on the scene a minute later.

'Who is it, Joe?' Her thin, reedy voice came whining from somewhere in the rear.

'It's my cousin from America,' answered Joe. 'Our Auntie Ellen's son.' He smiled broadly at Guy and stepped back, as if about to invite him in. But before Guy could step over the threshold, Morffyd appeared. She came towards them and halted at Joe's side, staring hard at Guy and sniffing suspiciously. Guy's warm smile and friendly greeting were ignored. For a long moment she eyed Guy with obvious distaste, then turned to her husband.

'What does he want here, then?'

Joe shrugged. 'Well, he says he's come to see us,' he said meekly.

'Yes. Yes, I've come to see you,' Guy echoed, meeker still.

'On the scrounge, are you boy?' Morffyd asked. 'You won't get anything here.'

'I – I haven't come to – to ask for anything – ' began Guy. 'I just want to – ' But quickly Morffyd cut in, saying, 'You're like all them foreigners. Think they can come over here and get something for nothing. Right, Joe?'

Joe answered at once. 'Right, Morffyd,' he said.

Morffyd was glaring at Guy. 'D'you know what we do with people like you?'

Guy continued to stand there, a wide, moronic, dying smile on his face. Whatever it was, he thought, it was certain to be something rather unpleasant. He was going to get no tea and crumpets here.

'Shall we show him, Joe?' With her words Morffyd turned and smiled at her husband, her smile showing two rows of the largest, whitest, most even false teeth that Guy had ever seen. The sight was terrifying.

'Call Fido,' she said.

As Joe stepped past him into the yard, and moved away out of sight, Guy reflected that Fido couldn't possibly be their son, not with such a name. Though not even that would surprise him now. Fighting to keep his sense of humour, and to bring a little lightness into the situation, he said lightly to the woman:

'Well, I don't want to wear my welcome out, as you British say . . . Ha ha.'

'No chance of that, boyoh,' Morffyd said. 'Here's our Fido coming.'

She gestured off and Guy turned to see Joe coming back across the yard, holding a dog on a leash.

'Shall we let him go, Joe?' Morffyd called out. 'What d'you reckon?'

Guy didn't wait for Joe's answer, but turned and, at a smart pace, started off for the gate. From behind him he heard the snarling of the dog, and Morffyd's voice.

'That's it – let him go, Joe. Let Fido go.' Then, as Guy quickened his pace: 'That's right. Go on now, Fido! See him off! Go for his throat!' Then to Guy as he dashed through the gate: 'Bugger off! Piss off! Dirty foreign scrounger! Go for his throat, Fido, boyoh!'

So here he was, sitting on the grass on the top of the hill, with Morffyd's voice still ringing in his ears.

Taking a ballpoint pen, Guy drew a quick line through the thirteenth name. There was just one name left. Aunt Mildred. That was if she was still living.

Guy looked at her address. According to the map it wasn't very far from here. And, supposing her to be alive, what kind of reception would he get there? He shrugged – well, maybe it wouldn't take long to find out.

Quickly he packed his flask, shouldered his pack, mounted his bicycle and rode away down the hill.

Aunt Mildred's dwelling was the prettiest that Guy had ever seen. For him it was the American idea of what a typical English country cottage should be. Beneath the thatched roof the white-washed walls were festooned with trailing ivy and climbing roses, while in the neat, green window-boxes blood-red geraniums nodded on their sturdy stems. Set in a half-acre of the most delightful garden imaginable, the little house looked like something dreamed up by an MGM movie set designer.

Raising his hand to knock on the door, Guy paused, and then let his hand fall back to his side. Somehow it was all too good to be true.

Supposing, he thought, supposing Aunt Mildred was as nutty as the rest of the bunch, what would he do . . . ? His silent question tailed off. He didn't think he could stand any more nerve-wracking experiences. And the dreadful thing was, he realised, such experiences were beginning to appear as the norm and not the exception. Would Aunt Mildred be any different? His mind went back to recall what little he knew of her – nothing except that she was a maiden lady in her late sixties who lived quite alone, and had done so for many years. There had been some little talk of her having once had a fiancé who had deserted her to go to New Zealand with another woman, but nothing else of even the slightest interest.

Still Guy paused. Oh, what the hell, he thought. Then aloud, said firmly:

'Here goes nothing,' and knocked the knocker.

After a few moments the door was opened by a petite, silver-haired lady. Standing in the cottage doorway, looking up at him, she wore a pale lilac dress and a neat white apron. The expression on her once-pretty face was gently quizzical. Just one look at her and Guy knew that this time it was going to be all right.

'Hello, Aunt Mildred,' he said, 'I'm your nephew, Guy.'

'Do have some more tea, Guy.'

'Thank you,' Guy said. 'I'd love some.'

Aunt Mildred took Guy's cup and poured in milk from the fine bone china jug, then added tea from the delicate rose-decorated teapot. 'Now tell me all about New York. I'm afraid I couldn't bear to live in a city that size. That threat of violence hanging over one all the time. I'm afraid I just close my eyes to those negative parts of our so-called civilization. I know my own existence is the epitome of parochialness, but it's sufficient. I am content.'

Between them the table was covered with a white cloth on which was spread a variety of foods: cheeses, ham, pickles, jams, home-made bread and cakes. Obviously Aunt Mildred took pride in the products of her kitchen. She smiled as Guy helped himself to more of the delicious home-made bread.

'Have some pickles, too.' Pots and jars were pushed across the table towards him. 'Here,' she said, 'there are gherkins, some nice mustard pickles, onions . . .'

Under her benevolent gaze Guy spooned out more pickles.

A gentle lull descended. Aunt Mildred faced him across the table, gently smiling, while outside in the afternoon sunshine the bees buzzed among the hollyhock blossoms.

'I think it was New York where Albert wanted to go first of all,' she said, almost as if speaking to herself. 'But then he decided that New Zealand offered the greater opportunities.'

'Albert?' said Guy.

'Albert, yes. Albert Collier. My fiancé.'

'Oh . . .' Guy nodded. Recalling the gossip, he was surprised that she could refer so easily to what must surely be a rather painful incident. Not knowing how to react he gave another half-nod, a half-smile, a half-shake-of-the-head, bit hard into a pickled onion and kept silent.

'He said he wanted to do the right thing.' Aunt Mildred snorted slightly. 'When he left me, I mean. *The right thing!* He said he didn't want to just – go off – like that – without telling me. He said he owed it to me – to tell me the truth. It was the *right thing* that I should know, he said. Huh.'

For a moment she sat gazing into her tea cup, clearly seeing some moment from the past. Then she said:

'Did you know that, Guy?'

'I beg your pardon . . . ?'

'Did you know that I was engaged to be married and that

my fiancé – turned from me – to – to another? Did you know that?'

Guy nodded. He felt a trifle embarrassed. 'Well,' he said, 'I had heard – *something* . . .'

'And why not?' Aunt Mildred said. 'It was no secret at the time. In fact it was the talk of the village.' She shifted her gaze and looked out over the geraniums to the distant hills. 'You know, I used to think Albert was the most handsome man I had ever seen.' She looked back at Guy. 'You remind me of him somewhat, you know. Same colouring . . . He was the son of a local farmer. Oh, such a charming young man. Oh, dear, yes, so charming.' She paused briefly, her lips set, then she went on:

'The girl was from the next village. A silly chit of a thing. I couldn't understand him. I was so much prettier. You might not believe me, Guy, but I was very pretty when I was young.'

'Oh, I'm sure . . .' Guy said.

'*She* wasn't pretty,' Aunt Mildred said. 'Oh, I suppose she had a kind of vulgar country charm, but that's all. Mind you, Albert always lacked taste. He must have. And I told him so the night he came to say goodbye. Oh, dear.' She shook her head. 'That was an awful scene, that was. But it was brave of him, I have to admit.' She gave a nod and then fell silent. Guy waited and, after a few moments, gently prompted her.

'Yes . . . ? What – what happened?'

'They were eloping, the fools. To New Zealand, so they said, and they'd just stopped off to tell me.'

She slapped at the tablecloth, making the china rattle. 'Can you believe such a thing? *Stopped off to tell me.* Those were the actual words he used.' She recovered her composure and dabbed daintily at her mouth with a linen napkin.

' "I'm in love with Marianne," that's what he told me. Just like that. That was her name – Marianne. And there she sat all the time, his little Marianne, simpering, gazing at him so adoringly. It was sickening. Sickening. And there *he* sat, just where you are now, drinking his tea, looking back at her with those great calf eyes. Sickening. But I kept cool – composed. I served tea and let him say what he'd come to say. Not once did I reproach him for his behaviour. No – I tried to be – civilized. And do you know – ' Here she came to an abrupt halt, and waved a slender white hand, as if dismissing it all. 'Oh, it's over, anyway,' she said with a sigh. 'It's all in the past.' She gave Guy a warm smile. 'And anyway, you don't want to sit here listening to the recollections of some silly, boring old woman.' Her chuckle was the gentlest sound. 'I'm sure you've had quite enough of me for one day.' She got to her feet and wagged a finger at him. 'I'm going to send you on your merry way now,' she said. 'But you must promise to come back and see me before you go on home to New York.'

'Uh – yes, I will,' Guy assured her. 'I'd love to.' He rose and pushed his chair back to the table. 'I've had a great afternoon. You can't imagine.'

Aunt Mildred looked up at him for a moment. 'You're a dear, sweet boy,' she said. She hesitated for a second, then turned, saying, 'Come along, before you go. I want to give you a few little things to take home with you. Some nice jam, perhaps ... a few little pickles ...' She moved away, starting towards the little hall. 'Come on, we'll go down to the cellar.'

Guy followed her from the room into the hall, then down a narrow flight of stairs to the cellar.

'Here we are ...'

After Aunt Mildred had switched on a light, Guy looked about him. The walls, he saw, were lined with shelves from floor to ceiling, and in the dim light from the single bulb he saw row upon row of jars and bottles of all shapes and sizes. So much food. Aunt Mildred, it seemed, could get carried away when it came to her pickles and preserves.

'Your pickling,' Guy said, indicating the many containers, 'it looks like you've made it into quite an art.'

'Oh, yes, indeed I have.' She nodded gravely. 'You could indeed say that. I've won awards for my pickles, you know.

Oh, yes. When I do a job I believe in doing it properly. No half measures for me.' She paused. 'Now – let's see . . .'

From a shelf nearby she took a cardboard box, and then from the cellar shelves began to take down various bottles and jars, packing them into the box. Watching her, Guy wondered how on earth he was going to carry it all. Aunt Mildred, seeing the doubtful look on his face, said brightly:

'You'll manage it all right, Guy. Big strong lad like you. And we can't have you going away empty-handed. Dear me. Whatever would your mother think? We want to make the right impression, don't we?'

The box was full. She gave a nod of satisfaction, a little conspiratorial smile and then thrust the laden box into his hands. 'You give these to your mother, with my best wishes,' she said. 'And tell her, as I said, that I'm famous for my pickles.'

Guy thanked her. She studied him judiciously for a moment, as if deliberating, then said, with a little laugh in her voice that threatened to bubble over, 'Guy, I like you – and I'm going to show you something else. Something that's secret.' From a shelf nearby she took a lamp, switched it on and, beckoning to him to follow, turned and led the way to towards a door that was almost hidden in a shadowy corner.

Stopping at the door she took a key from her pocket and inserted it into the lock. 'Now you're going to see something,' she said, her voice slightly hushed, touched with a note of awe. 'I wouldn't show just anyone but, well – you *are* one of the family.'

She turned the key, opened the door and led the way into a smaller, darker room. Guy followed. Inside, it took a few seconds for his eyes to become accustomed to the deep shadows, and in his temporary blindness he almost stumbled over a bundle of old rags that lay in his path.

'Careful,' Aunt Mildred said, and raised the lamp to aid his vision.

Guy stared aghast.

The bundle of rags moved beneath his gaze, and a thin,

scrawny arm reached out to him. In the lamp's dim light Guy saw the figure of an old man, indescribably ragged and dirty. He was chained to a large ring set in the stone wall, his grey hair, like his beard, hanging matted and unkempt.

'Oh, that's Albert,' said Aunt Mildred. 'I should have warned you about him.'

'Did you – did you say – *Albert*?'

'Yes. My fiancé – I told you about him.' She glanced down at the shambolic wreck. 'I think perhaps I should shorten his chain.'

With his mouth open, Guy watched as Aunt Mildred's erstwhile fiancé crawled towards her, one arm stretched out. Seeing the look on Guy's face, Aunt Mildred said, 'Not a pretty sight, is he? And he used to take such pride in himself.' She shook her head, and added: 'But take no notice of him. He's always trying to get attention. Never mind him – look at this.'

Guy watched then as she grasped the door handle of a large cupboard and pulled open the door.

'There,' she said proudly, raising the lamp higher. 'What do you think of that?'

Guy peered closer, frowning in puzzlement at an enormous glass jar that almost filled the cupboard. It was not easy to see so well in the gloom, but the jar seemed to contain some large white, oddly-shaped mass. At his shoulder Aunt Mildred's voice was hushed, faintly apologetic.

'I had to double her up like that. She wouldn't have gone in otherwise.'

And then Guy saw what the thing was.

In the cloudy, yellowish-green liquid hung the naked body of a young woman. Trussed up into a tortuous, unnatural position, she hung suspended, her dull, wide eyes lifelessly gazing out at her viewers.

'Marianne was my best pickle,' Aunt Mildred said, a faint note of pride in her voice.

Behind them, Albert Collier made a feeble attempt to speak, and Aunt Mildred quickly turned to him and snapped out:

'Be quiet! Can't you see I've got company.' To Guy she said, 'I do apologize.' She turned back to study Albert for a few seconds then said casually: 'I must say he's lasted rather well – all things considered. More than I can say for Marianne. She didn't last more than a few months. No stamina.'

Albert was trying to speak again, his mouth opening wide, showing blackened tooth stumps. The sound that issued from his slobbering lips was a long, whining groan.

'You know what, Guy – ?' Aunt Mildred laid a gentle hand on her nephew's arm, her lips pursed. 'Sometimes I ask myself, what*ever* did I see in him.'

PAT-A-CAKE, PAT-A-CAKE

I LIKE IT here in this place. It's warm and cosy. And the people around me are nice. The face on the dark-haired lady who leans over my cot is especially nice. She has the softest brown eyes. I kept stealing little glances at her as she tucked me in with this beautiful new Rupert Bear eiderdown. I never had anything like this before. It's really nice. Not that I could *tell* them, of course – the man or the woman. Well, I *could* tell them, but they just wouldn't understand, and I've learned now that it's quite useless to try – no matter how clear I make myself. I think it must be something they learn – an ability they develop as we grow older and bigger. I hope so. I hope they will learn. There's so much I want to tell them.

I think this place is going to be my new home. Just now the woman leaned over me and said: 'You're going to stay here with your daddy and me for ever and ever.' Oh, I felt so glad. It's exactly what I wanted. I would have hugged her except that my arms aren't long enough. So I sort of clapped my hands instead. Just think – these two people are going to be my new mummy and daddy. They must be.

I had a mummy before. But the new one is much nicer. I never had a daddy before, though. I must say I like it. This one's got a very faint tobacco-y smell about him. I can recognize it. But it's not unpleasant, and his voice is very kind and gentle. I wonder if all daddies are like him.

I'm going to stay here. I shall. I don't think I'll ever move on again. It's so nice.

I just clapped my hands together again, and the lady – I must always try to think of her as *Mummy* – went all smiley and happy. She said to me: 'That's it! Clever boy! That's it – Pat-a-cake, pat-a-cake, baker's man ... Go on ... Pat-a-cake, pat-a-cake, baker's man.' So I clapped my hands together even harder – as well as I could – and gave her a big grin. She laughed then, and said again:

> Pat-a-cake, pat-a-cake, baker's man,
> Bake me a cake as fast as you can.
> Pat it and prick it and mark with B,
> And put it in the oven for baby and me!

I think that's how it went. Mind you, I'm not absolutely sure what this pat-a-cake thing is. I think it must be this clapping thing I do – waving my arms around – things like that. Though I'm not all that good at it yet – the clapping, pat-a-cake thing, I mean. It's not always easy to make your hands actually *meet* – hit together, you understand. The new mummy seems to know this, and she took my hands and held them and gently clapped them together. And all the time she sang about pat-a-cake. I suppose I shall get the hang of it all sooner or later. I hope so. Some people do seem to set such store by these funny things, and I would so like to please her. And Daddy, too. I wonder what a baker's man is . . . I expect I'll find that out some time as well.

That must have been what I did with my first mummy – the pat-a-cake, I mean. Well, something like it.

My first mummy. She was my *real* mummy. I didn't like her.

I'm not proud of it. Because she was my real mummy, after all. But she was quite horrid. I've no idea where a daddy was – if there was one. There was just her. And me. Well, sometimes there were other men around – strangers who'd stay for an odd night or so in her bed – but no one I ever got to like. Oh, I'm so glad I'm not with her any more.

This lady now, this *new* mummy, calls me nice names like – like *baby*, and – *sweetheart*, and *darling*, and other things, and the way she says them they sound *nice*. I can tell she's smiling even when I can't see her face. You see, her smile is in her voice. But the other mummy – the real one – she didn't call me nice things. She used to call me things like *bloody kid*, and *bastard*, and *snivelling little sod*. And they didn't sound nice. Not at all. Not the way she said them.

My nose is always clean now. It wasn't before. Before, I often had a runny nose. That mother never bothered at all. Once I got up all my courage and said to her: 'How would you like it if *your* nose was never wiped . . .' But she just said: 'I'll bloody well goo-goo-goo you in a minute!' Oh, it's best to forget her.

My new mummy and daddy are both near me now. *He* just looked down at me. His smile is so wide. He put a hand to my face. And I flinched. I didn't mean to. But his hand turned out to be the softest, gentlest touch you ever felt. So I put my hand up and held on to his thumb. He looked so pleased that I held on even harder. He likes that a lot. It's funny: it's very easy to make some people happy. The new mummy said:

'Look, Dave, look at the little love . . .'

She never talked like that – the first one.

But I won't think about her. I said I wouldn't. I shall just think about these two. They love me. You can tell; it's easy. They're nice. I think these are the two I would have chosen if I'd had any choice, any say in the matter. I think it's a great pity that babies have to put up with what they get in the way of parents. I mean, without any thought or consideration at all I just got dumped with that awful woman who swore all the time, and who had nicotine-stained fingers and bad teeth. And her breath was really terrible. Not that she ever kissed me or anything, I'm glad to say. Most of the time she just left me sitting there in this terrible battered old pram she got from somewhere. And I could be really *filthy*, honestly, and she wouldn't bother in the least. She used to go out to the pub and play darts most evenings, sometimes with one or other of the men who came to the door. Or else she'd go to Bingo. It didn't make much difference to me. Wherever she went, I'd be left. For ages and ages and ages. Sometimes with the woman who lived next door and sometimes – mostly – on my own. Yes, I think it's really unfair that we can't choose our own mummy and daddy.

I remember thinking that first of all when I was sitting outside the supermarket one day – in my pram. And I was looking at some of the other babies around me. They were so clean and smelt so lovely. And you should have seen some of the mummies and daddies – *beautiful*. Absolutely. And I thought then – how unfair it all was. I felt really ashamed. There I was, covered with this disgusting, dirty old blanket (not like my Rupert Bear eiderdown), and feeling very uncomfortable because I hadn't been changed for ages and I decided, then and there, that I had to do something about it. It couldn't go on. I mean, it just couldn't, could it?

My new daddy just said to my new mummy:

'That scar on his arm. Look. Poor little chap. Really must have hurt him. Fancy burning a kid like that – I mean, accident or no accident. Still, the doctor says it'll fade in time . . .'

They mean that mark where she spilt boiling milk over me from the saucepan. Honest, I just wasn't safe. I *had* to get out.

Anyway, as I said, I'd made up my mind. Now I just had to wait for the right chance. And the right time. And I had to think of a good way. And there weren't that many ways open to me, still being on the little side as people go. But I was sure there'd be something.

All this, of course, was still outside the supermarket. And I didn't have much chance to think on the problem then, as she came out loaded down with groceries. The next second I was almost smothered under a whole heap of instant mashed potatoes, tinned beans and tinned spaghetti and sliced bread. I said, before I could stop myself:

'For goodness' sake have a bit of consideration, will you? I mean, I'm not made of *rubber!*'

And she said, crossly: 'Don't you start bleedin' cryin', you little misery. If you've got wind it's your own bloody fault. I wish to Christ I'd never 'ad you.'

You can see what I was up against. One felt totally impotent. And it was just so hard to get anything across to anyone. I remember once when I was in my pram outside an off-licence one lunchtime. This policeman came by and stopped and crouched down by me. He said: 'Hello, young fellow. Waiting for your mother, are you? She won't be long.'

I thought, now's my chance. I said to him:

'Look at the state I'm in. You wouldn't believe it but I've had this nappy on since last night. *Last night!* And she doesn't care. Not a bit. Do you suppose you could report the matter to the proper authorities when you get an opportunity . . . ? Do you think you could help to get me moved to someone else? Another mummy? As you can see, things are just not working out as they are . . . Please . . . ?'

I didn't have a chance to say any more as *she* came out of the shop carrying all the bottles. The policeman stood up as she approached and smiled at her.

'I think he's getting impatient for you,' he said. He turned back to me and put his face close up to mine. 'Go on,' he said. 'Go on, say it. Mum-mum-mum-mum-mum-mum. You'll be talking next, won't you. Mum-mum-mum-mum.'

I dribbled and made a rude noise.

That night we went to the pub. It was her darts night. She wheeled me into the shadow of the wall that I knew so well, grabbed her darts and her handbag and went off inside. I was left alone. Just like that.

It's a good job it was summer. Honestly, I could have frozen to death, otherwise, for all the notice she took of me. I was there for ages and she never once even looked out to see that I was all right. One time some strange woman with breath that smelt of beer and onions came out and stuck her face close to mine. She turned and yelled back through the open pub door:

'Yeh, 'e's all right, love . . .'

All right . . . ? I tell you. There I was, hungry, thirsty, miserable and dirty. I hadn't been changed still. The least she could have done was given me a clean nappy. I mean, supposing I'd got knocked down.

God, it was boring out there. I had a bit of a chat with a dog for a few minutes, a collie crossed with a spaniel; not the most communicative breed at the best of times, but at least it broke the monotony for a while. Later on, the beery-oniony woman came again and looked at me. I said to her as plainly as I could: 'Would you ask her if we can go home, please? Tell her I'm tired and bored, will you? And I'm so *wet*, I want to be *changed*. Please . . .'

A look of real concern flashed across the woman's face for a second, and I thought, at last I've got through to somebody. Then she said: 'That's it, darlin'. You cough it up.' Then she patted me on the back. I ask you – what can you do . . . ?

Anyway, at last *she* came out. She flung her stuff on the pram and started to wheel me up the street. And looking out I saw this man there, walking along with her. He wasn't what I'd call nice, though. Not like *this* daddy. But they were talking and talking. We stopped outside the fish and chip shop where the light was very bright and got in my eyes. She braked the pram and joined the end of the queue leading to the counter; the man went with her. They didn't take any notice of me at all, and didn't even look to see what I was up to. Of course, by this time I was really awake. What with all that noise in my ears and that light in my eyes I couldn't very well be expected to sleep, could I. Actually it's a good job I didn't. Otherwise I might still be with her today.

I thought she'd never come back to the pram. It seemed ages before I felt her shadow over me and smelt the smell of her – chips, fish and vinegar all mixed up with the beer. I had my eyes closed now and I heard her say:

'Oh, bloody 'ell. Look what the little bastard's gone and done.' She had a really ugly voice, and her voice got nearer and louder, and angrier. And all the time I kept my face turned away. 'He's emptied every bleedin' thing out of my 'andbag,' she said. 'Look at that bleedin' mess.'

And then she leaned down, right low, over the pram. And that's when I did the pat-a-cake. But I did it against her neck and as hard as I could. It wasn't easy to aim properly – I'm not that good, as you'd probably guess – but this time I got it *just right*. And the next thing she was straightening up, and clasping her hands to her throat, and I got a sudden glimpse of the red coming out between her fingers. She half shouted, half spoke: 'Oh, my God, what's that little sod done to me? Jesus Christ, I'm *bleedin'*, for God's sake!'

The man went up next to her then and I could see him putting up his hands, trying to stop the blood coming out of her neck. But he couldn't. Of course he couldn't. No one could. And all the time her cries were getting louder and more frightened. Lots of people started gathering around us – I think it must be the blood that does it – and all talking at once. You should have seen and heard all the panic going on.

'Quick! Quick!' somebody was shouting, ' – it's the jugular vein. She's bleeding to death!'

And then more voices: 'Get a tourniquet! That's what she needs.'

'What for?'

'To stop the bleeding – !'

' – A tourniquet? Round her neck?'

'It'll stop the bleeding.'

'Yeh! – stop her breathin' as well.'

You should have been there, seen them all running around. I was the only calm one there and for a good few minutes nobody took any notice of me ... and all the time I still had the darts in my hand. Then this strange woman came over and took them away from me. She did it anxiously but quite gently.

'Let's have these before you do any more damage,' she said. 'We don't want *you* hurt as well.' Her face was close as she bent down to me. She looked very sad. She murmured softly: '*Poor* little devil ...'

'Listen,' I said, looking up into her eyes, 'I had to do it. I *had* to. I mean, what kind of a future did I have with her ...?'

The woman shook her head. 'Ah, listen to him chortling away,' she said. 'Poor little bugger. Aw, bless 'im. Poor little darlin' thinks it's all a huge joke. Thank God he's too young to understand what he's done . . .'

And that's when I *really* started to laugh. I mean, honest – I just had to.

MY VERY GOOD FRIEND

T HERE was no doubt about it, the insect had grown. Not only did it look larger, but, Pierre could tell, holding it gently in the palm of his hand, that it was also heavier.

Studying the slender green creature, Pierre experienced a sensation of great pride and satisfaction. After all his months of research he was finally seeing results. At last there was something to show for all those hours spent bending over his workbench in his small – almost primitive – laboratory. His early failures – and there had been so many of them – counted for nothing now in the face of his success.

Briefly he let his mind stray back into the past, seeing the seemingly-endless succession of ill-fated creatures that had been the subjects for his experiments. There had been so many: the flies, the yellow-jackets, the bees, the mosquitoes. And all of them had failed the test – not one had survived for more than a very short time.

So he had gone on, making changes here, alterations there.

The drug he had developed, and now used, was quite different from the one he had started with. And as luck would have it, just as it, the drug, came to be perfected, he had found the praying mantises.

Like his earlier subjects, the first ones had succumbed, but the next one – and what a time that was! – had survived for several weeks after the initial treatment.

And now here he was with the fifth praying mantis. And after five weeks of continuous treatment it still showed no signs of weakening or deterioration. On the contrary, it seemed positively to glow with health – if it was possible for such a very green creature to glow. The rate of its growth was accelerating day by day, Pierre had noticed. He smiled; he had known that he could do it – would do it – eventually.

He replaced the creature in the small, mesh-covered cage he had made for it, then watched as the insect devoured a bluebottle that had been provided for its lunch. When the meal was finished the mantis turned its head and gazed at Pierre with strange, unfathomable eyes. It was uncanny, that, Pierre thought, how it could actually swivel its head from side to side, unlike most other insects. But there, the praying mantis was an extraordinary creature altogether.

Pierre never tired of studying the insect. He found that he could sit for hours, gazing with rapt fascination, just staring at it. And it was not known as a praying mantis for nothing; it even adopted its praying attitude whilst eating. Pierre found it the most enthralling of all his subjects and he looked upon it with a profoundly respectful air, completely caught up in its mystery.

It *was* a mystery to him, too. Coming from Paris to the backwoods of America he had never seen a praying mantis before. Consequently he had been intrigued by the small, delicate-looking creature from the moment he had first seen one – sitting on a twig outside the laboratory. Mesmerized, he had watched as the insect had snatched a small aphid from a nearby leaf and quickly devoured it.

Now, however, the smaller insects were no longer sufficient to supply the nutritional needs of the swiftly-growing creature before him. Its diet now consisted of the larger species – flies, moths, butterflies, etc. From an approximate length of one and a half inches the praying mantis now measured well over three. Soon, Pierre reckoned, he'd be able actually to inject the growth-giving serum – instead of brushing it onto the bodies of the insects that had been caught for the creature's food.

With a satisfied sigh, Pierre turned off the light over the cage and stepped outside on to the veranda of the small house. He looked out over acres of woodland – only one other house visible among the trees. The owner of that house, Royston

Stevens, was the only human he saw from one week to another. Apart from the occasional visits from his American neighbour, Pierre was entirely alone.

But this was the way he wanted it. This was the way it suited him. Never a gregarious person, he had at once welcomed the solitude of this place. It had accepted him and he had embraced its silence, its solitude, knowing instinctively that it was right for him. Here he was free from the inquisitive glances of strangers, the half-fascinated, half-shocked glances that would be thrown in his direction.

In the shadowed glass of the kitchen window he saw, for a second, the image of his reflection. It gazed back at him, a slight, deformed figure with stunted legs and distorted features. His face had something of the appearance of a clay model, one side of which might have been forcibly dragged down in a fit of sudden anger. The face was ugly – shocking sometimes even to Pierre himself who had grown up with it. Only the eyes were beautiful. Soft, limpid, infinitely kind and gentle, they shone, a clear, deep blue, twin oases in the desert of his ugliness.

Quickly he turned his head away – he could never look at himself for long.

When Royston Stevens visited the house a week later he found Pierre in the back yard, hard at work on the construction of a large cage which he was covering with a coarse wire mesh. After their initial greetings Stevens asked:

'What's that for?'

For a long moment Pierre just looked at him, inwardly debating whether or not to impart the details of his wonderful secret. Then in the end he beckoned and led the way into his laboratory.

'There. Look at that,' he said proudly in his French-accented English.

Stevens looked towards the smaller cage on the workbench and gasped.

'But . . . what is it?'

Pierre smiled – he couldn't help himself. 'What does it look like?' he asked in return.

'It's – it's like an enormous – praying mantis.'

Pierre nodded. 'True.'

'Jesus . . . !' Stevens moved nearer to the cage, gazing in a kind of sick fascination at the huge insect before him.

'I call him Emil,' Pierre said, grinning widely.

The mantis was now well over a foot in length and clearly would very soon be too large for the confines of its present home. The body of the insect was a brilliant green with a bright sheen on the skin. It sat there, as always, its short, powerful forearms held together in their attitude of prayer. 'How . . . ?' was all that Stevens managed to say.

Later, over coffee, Pierre related the story of his experiments.

'Don't you realise what this will mean to the world?' Pierre asked excitedly. 'Do you realise that humanity need never hunger again?'

Looking at the ugly face before him, the American silently framed the question: *Why are you so concerned for humanity when you can't even face it? And anyway, what has it ever done for you . . . ?* Then, aloud, he said, 'It's wonderful, Pierre. It's wonderful.'

Later they looked again at Emil.

'I can see why you're building a bigger cage,' Stevens said.

'Yes. Emil must have room to move around. He must be comfortable.'

'Why do you call him Emil?'

The Frenchman shrugged. 'I used to have a dog. He was Emil.'

'How do you know this one's male?'

'I don't.'

'You don't?'

Pierre spread his hands. 'Well, I've no experience of them – other than this one, and in the little researching I've done I haven't come up with any really helpful information. I read somewhere that the female has a shorter wing span, and that with some species the colour of the abdomen is a little different – but . . .' He laughed. 'What's it matter, anyway? If I find Emil's a lady I shall change her name. To *Emilie*.'

And so Emil grew. Two weeks later Pierre moved the insect into the larger cage which he had placed on the veranda. The praying mantis now measured over three feet in height, and the drug for its growth was administered directly by injection. Pierre wondered whether he should perhaps stop giving the drug – but no, he couldn't. Not now. Having seen his experiment working so successfully he felt compelled to continue.

Pierre never tired of gazing at his pet (he had ceased to think of Emil merely as the subject of an experiment), and spent many long hours sitting or standing before the cage, observing the enormous creature within. As he approached the cage, Pierre would see the large, intelligent-looking head turn to watch him. Those eyes that looked into his own were filled with trust.

Feeding times were a source of endless fascination. Pierre had taken now to trapping birds and then releasing them into the confines of the cage. The praying mantis would turn its head, attracted by the frantic fluttering, the keen eyes watching, studying as the terrified bird sought a means of escape. Apart from the slow, measured movement of the head, Emil's body would be quite still, absolutely motionless, as if carefully judging the distance between itself and its prey. And then, suddenly, without warning, Emil would go into action. The forelegs would shoot out – so swiftly that their movement was, to Pierre's eyes, just a blur – and the unsuspecting bird would be snatched up, caught in the strong, unrelenting grasp, and carried to the large waiting jaws.

Pierre always had to look away at this point. He found it impossible to watch as the birds were devoured. The fact that they were killed at all brought him considerable distress but, he reasoned with himself, it was necessary. All God's creatures had to live – and live in the only way they knew.

With Pierre, Emil was gentleness itself. Quite without fear, the Frenchman could go right into the cage. There he would stand, talking to his pet, whispering his soft, soothing words. He would stroke the neck of the large green creature, and the trusting eyes would watch him, following his every move.

Pierre found that, within himself, a great fondness, a great love, was growing for his pet. There was a rapport here that he had never experienced before.

As time went on Emil began to wait anxiously for Pierre's coming. Seeing him approach the bars of the cage the insect would hurry towards him, tiny piercing cries issuing from its wide mouth. Pierre, hearing the sounds, seeing the eagerness, would feel his heart leap with joy and affection. Here was a living creature who never noticed his deformities. The eyes of the praying mantis never flinched when they lighted on its jailer. Instead they studied him with devotion. It was a mutual love and trust, and Pierre gloried in it.

'What happened to your insect friend?'

Royston Stevens sat opposite Pierre over their coffee cups. There had been no mention of Emil since the American's arrival some fifteen minutes earlier, and he was burning with curiosity.

Pierre smiled. It had been some weeks since the two men had last met and he was quite sure that Stevens had not visited him merely for his coffee – good though it was.

'Come. I will show you.' Pierre arose and led the way on to the back porch. There, inside the cage, was the praying mantis.

'My God!' Stevens cried, aghast. He stared open-mouthed at the enormous creature that crouched there and turned its head to study him with cool, impassioned eyes.

'It's – it's grotesque!'

'No.' Pierre frowned, then murmuring, 'Beautiful, beautiful,' he moved to the cage and thrust an arm through between the bars.

'Emil ... Emil.' He crooned the name softly, seductively, and Stevens watched as the huge praying mantis moved eagerly towards the outstretched hand.

'You see?' Pierre asked the gaping American. 'There is nothing grotesque about him. Grotesque? How can you say such a thing?' He began to stroke the creature's head, Emil clearly revelling in the sensation.

'How can you bear to touch him?' Stevens asked. 'Aren't you afraid?'

'Afraid?' Pierre laughed at the idea. 'He's tame,' he said. 'Can't you see? He loves me. We understand one another.' And seeing the look of horrified doubt on the American's face, he added: 'Watch.'

Slipping up the catch, Pierre pushed open the door and went inside. Stevens moved closer, watching intently.

'Emil is my friend,' Pierre said, smiling through the bars, his eyes crinkling. 'My very good friend. Our relationship is based on trust and love. Emil trusts me. Emil loves me.'

Stevens forced himself to try to relax. He tried a smile in return. 'I'm sure you're right,' he said. 'But you must admit it's bound to give anybody a bit of a shock.'

'Ah, yes, of course,' said Pierre. 'But that's because you don't know my Emil.' He reached out and ran one gentle caressing hand down the long green length of the insect's huge body. Under his touch Emil gave a small shudder of delight and moved closer to him.

Pierre continued to stroke his friend and after a few moments Emil's head began to turn, slowly moving from side to side – from left to right – right to left, giving the creature the appearance of a huge green puppet.

'I think perhaps you might be female after all,' Pierre chuckled, smoothing the bright skin. 'I think perhaps I should have called you Emilie.' His hand moved faster now, like butterflies on the sensitive body, fluttering, titillating, and Emil's head moved quicker in response.

Stevens, watching in fascination, saw the enormous creature give a tremendous wriggle of joy. There was something almost obscene and disgusting about the spectacle before him, yet he found it impossible to look away. He gazed enthralled as the praying mantis – easily a foot taller than Pierre – throbbed and pulsated to the touch of the Frenchman's hand.

'Pierre . . . Pierre,' he said, a note of urgency in his voice, 'I think you should come out.'

'What? Nonsense! ' Pierre said, laughing. 'Emil – *Emilie* – is *enjoying* herself! I told you, she *loves* me.'

The body of the praying mantis seemed now to be quivering in an ecstasy of sensual delight. Stevens saw the creature's form arch, then straighten, then arch again, and he knew quite suddenly, beyond any shadow of doubt, that the insect was indeed female. And, just as certainly, he knew that the innocent, unknowing Pierre had become more to her than just a very good friend.

The movements of the creature now became more frantic in appearance, taking on the aspect of some ancient, ritualistic dance.

And suddenly Pierre became afraid.

With his own realisation of the sex of his captive he saw the weird gyrations in a new light – the praying mantis was doing some kind of mating dance. Memory flooded back to him of things read – things he had thought were forgotten. He gave a terrified scream and backed away towards the door of the cage.

But Emilie followed, reaching out for him. And catching him, she clutched him and clasped him to her. Held in the creature's powerful embrace, Pierre felt a violent shudder shake his lover's huge green form. Desperately he struggled, and with a strength born of desperation, tore himself from her grasp and made a lunge for the door. Even though he reached it, however, there was no room for him to open it inwards. He screamed again, his eyes starting from their sockets as, in his abject terror, he gazed at Stevens, beseeching his help.

But there was no time. As Stevens looked about for something with which to ward off the attack, Emilie was moving in again.

Pierre fought desperately, struggling with the door, but in another moment his great lover was upon him. Her two short but immensely powerful arms snapped out, tightly grasped him and clutched him to her.

Emilie was simply behaving true to her instincts.

Held fast in his deathly sweetheart's embrace, Pierre gave a scream. Even as he did so, Emilie's jaws descended, gaping above him. Pierre opened his mouth to scream again but the hard, horny mouth had clamped over his face, stopping all further sound.

Emilie's shining eyes never lost their look of love as she wrenched off his head.

SAMHAIN

Wearing her track suit, Doris stood gasping for breath as the lift took her up to the fifth floor, the top of the apartment building. A minute later at the door of the flat she discovered that she'd come out without her keys and she rang the bell and waited impatiently for Arthur to answer. Then at last, after the fourth ring, the door was opened. She helped it aside with an angry shove and stepped into the hall.

'Arthur,' she gasped (she still hadn't got her breath back), 'didn't you hear me ringing?'

He shook his head. 'No, I'm sorry, dear; I was in the bedroom going through my underwear. You know – I think I need to get some more.'

'You need to get a hearing aid, that's what you need.' With her words she turned away and strode into the kitchen where she poured herself a glass of water. She would have liked a Coke but there was no sense in half killing yourself to take off a few pounds and then put it all straight back on again. As she stood there slowly sipping the water Arthur came to the open doorway and stood looking at her with the inane smile that always infuriated her so.

'How was the running?' he asked.

Her answer was clipped, cold. 'If you mean the jogging, it was fine.'

'Yes. Yes, of course – jogging.' He nodded. 'I have to hand it to you – you've got more energy than I have. If *I* tried a run round the park I'd be dead before I got halfway.'

It's a pity you don't try it then, a voice inside her head snapped, *and save me all the trouble you're putting me to.* She kept silent, though, and turned and rinsed the empty glass under the tap.

As she dried the glass and put it away Arthur said solicitously, 'I'll bet you're hungry, are you? Would you like me to make you some breakfast?'

'You?' She looked at him with contempt. 'You know very well you're useless in the kitchen. You're as incompetent there as you are everywhere else.' She paused. 'Besides, I'm trying to lose weight, you know that. I've got some pride – even if you haven't.'

He looked hurt. 'What does that mean?'

'It means it wouldn't hurt *you* to lose a few pounds, either. You do know what this weekend is, don't you?'

He nodded. 'Of course. The thirty-first. Halloween.'

'*Halloween?*' There was disgust in her tone. 'Yes, that's what *they* call it, those idiots out there.' She gestured with an impatient hand, taking in the rest of the world. '*I* prefer to call it by its proper name.'

'Samhain?'

'Of *course* Samhain.'

'All right – Samhain – but so what?'

She made a short, mocking sound of derision. '*So what?* he asks. *So what?* Maybe it doesn't bother you, the thought of stripping off and dancing around in the nude in front of all our friends. Maybe you don't give it a second thought. Maybe you're happy with your body the way it is. If so, then you've got a lot to be happy about – because there's a lot of it. Personally, if it were me, I'd want to do something about it.'

He frowned. 'Oh, come on, Doris, what can I do about it? I'm fifty-six years old. I'm not a young man anymore. Besides, there'll be plenty there older than I am. Plenty.'

He looked hurt and she gave a sigh. 'Oh – forget it, Arthur. I won't say anything else. It doesn't make any difference anyway. You never listen.'

She pushed past him and went into the lounge where she flopped down into her easy chair, took off her shoes, put her feet up on the footstool and closed her eyes. After a few moments she heard him come into the room, and then she heard his voice again, irritatingly considerate as always:

'Are you asleep?'

Without opening her eyes she said, 'Of course I'm not asleep.'

'I just wondered.' A pause. 'Would you like a cup of coffee?'

She opened her eyes, about to say no, then gave a grudging shrug. 'Yes, why not. If you think you can manage it.'

'Doris, of course I can manage it.' He started off across the room. 'You want it black?'

'Of course black. I always have it black.'

'Yes, of course.'

She turned her head and watched his thick, heavy body move through the doorway, then she sighed, got to her feet and stretched. There was a mirror near the window and she stepped in front of it and looked at herself. She didn't look at all bad for her forty-three years, she thought. And holding herself like this – erect and with her stomach drawn in – she looked *years* younger. Trouble was, it was impossible to sustain the effort. You forgot, and with the forgetting everything sagged again. She must get into the habit of holding herself well; work on her posture as well as everything else. After all, soon she'd be free again . . .

As she looked at her reflection she thought again of the thirty-first. Tomorrow. Everything depended on tomorrow. Tomorrow would see the end to her problems and the beginning of a new life. And the day would bring other bonuses too: at the meeting she'd see that young male witch, the new initiate from Lyddiard, Steve Walker. She hadn't seen him since the initiation ceremony back at the end of April, the Feast of Beltane, but she remembered him well enough: tall, tanned, good-looking and with an obvious taste for older women. Not that she regarded herself as old, Satan forbid, but when he was only in his late twenties one had to acknowledge the age difference. Thinking of him now she remembered how he had smiled at her – and in such a very special way. He'd had his clothes on then, of course, but even so they hadn't been able to disguise the firmness, the clean, muscular lines of his body. Not like Arthur with his pale flab.

She pictured Arthur as he'd be at the dance – as usual making a complete idiot of himself. Some people had no dignity at all. Well, at least *she* knew how to go on. And when *she* danced nobody was going to snigger or look the other way. With the thought she did a couple of steps in front of the mirror. It looked good – and *she* looked pretty good too – a damned sight better than that stupid Shirley Goldberg. Sure Shirley Goldberg's figure was a lot firmer and more up-together these days – but so it should be – she'd spent enough on cosmetic surgery. And it showed, of course. There was no way of disguising those scars. Those scars – good Satan, in the cold weather Shirley Goldberg looked as if she'd been pressed against a wire fence.

Arthur came back into the room then and she sat down and took the cup of coffee he handed her. Looking down at it, she said impatiently, 'I said *black,* Arthur. Can't you ever get anything right?'

As he moved back to the kitchen with the offending cup of coffee she reflected on her loathing of him. And it would never change now, she knew that – which was one reason she had decided to get rid of him and look out for a newer model. Well, she had to. They couldn't go on as they were. With him around she had no future at all. Oh, yes, she could leave him, of course – but what good would that do? She'd just be giving up her home in this flat to go and find someplace on her own – and someplace not nearly as comfortable – and almost certainly she'd have to get a job of some kind too. No, she couldn't afford to leave Arthur – and as she couldn't bear the thought of continuing to live with him either, then there was only one thing to be done.

Which she was in the process of taking care of right now. And so much trouble it was, too. She had never dreamed. All those sessions in the coven's library for a start, doing all that research. It was mind-blowingly tedious – but it was the only way to do things, she had no doubt of that.

Thinking of the library, she thought of the books she'd

been studying. It hadn't been easy getting access to them. It had surprised her just how closely they were guarded. She had told the coven librarian that she was taking a degree course on the ancient arts. And he had believed her, the fool. She remembered his grave expression as he had brought the old, leather-bound volumes and placed them before her. 'Be careful with them, won't you?' he had said. 'And do remember that they mustn't be taken out of this room. We wouldn't want them falling into the wrong hands, would we? If that happened, there's no telling where the mischief would stop.'

Mischief. *Mischief* – it seemed such a pathetic little word when applied to the act of murder. Not that anyone was going to construe it as murder. It would be put down to heart failure. Simple. She smiled to herself. And now her researches were finished, and she had all the answers she wanted. And now, too, she had the stone and the nail. And this evening she'd have the clay portrait as well.

After a few moments Arthur approached with a fresh cup of coffee – black this time – in his hand. As she took it from him she said, 'I'll be out this evening, you haven't forgotten that, have you?'

'Oh, yes, of course.' He nodded. 'Your art class. I wasn't sure that you'd still be going – what with the feast and everything tomorrow.'

Still going? 'Of course I'm still going,' she said witheringly. Wild horses wouldn't keep her away.

'How are you getting on?' he asked.

'Fine. I'm getting on fine.'

'You must really enjoy it, your clay modelling – these past few weeks you've been so keen.'

She shrugged. 'Yes – I do enjoy it.'

'Maybe I could come with you one evening. It might be interesting.'

She tried to picture him in the art studio, making a hash of everything. What an embarrassment he would be. 'Oh, I don't think it would appeal to you at all,' she said.

'Oh . . . What are you making?'

'This and that.'

'What, exactly?'

'I've been modelling a figure.'

'All this time? Just one? It must be huge.'

'No – it's quite small.'

'But it's been weeks.'

'I've been trying to get it right.'

'I see. And are you nearly there, you think?'

'Nearly there. This evening it'll be finished.'

'Well, that's nice.'

Well, that's nice, the voice in her head mimicked. *You wouldn't think it was so nice if you knew whose figure I was modelling, you old fool.* She wondered for a moment how he would react if she told him that the model was of *him* . . . She frowned momentarily at the thought of her work in the class. Getting his likeness had proved so difficult. It would have been easy if she had some real artistic ability – but she hadn't and that was it. Anyway, after several poor starts she'd been getting on better over the past few sessions and now, this evening, at last, it would be done.

The idea for the clay model was one of the things she'd got from her researches in the library. Not that such means were that secret. On the contrary, she supposed it must be one of the most commonly known methods of disposing of someone. Even so, however, she didn't intend relying on some half-baked old wives' tales handed down; she meant to get it right – which was why she'd gone to the experts.

And that, too, was why she had chosen the thirty-first – that was the day when the spells would be at their most potent. Strange, really, she thought, most people today had no idea what the day really meant – and what it had meant since early times. *Samhain* – that was the real meaning of the thirty-first of October. Samhain, one of the two great witches' festivals of the year – a celebration of fire and the dead and the powers of darkness. In the modern world the thirty-first was generally recognized only as All Hallows' Eve, and celebrated only by children with turnip lanterns, silly masks, games and dressing up. Still, it could be worse, she supposed; in America they made even more nonsense out of the whole thing with their ridiculous trick-or-treating. Huh – if any children came to *her* door carrying bags of flour or whatever and begging for sweets, they'd get something they weren't prepared for, the little monsters. Mind you, that's what came from too much civilization. Thank Satan England hadn't gone *that* far – *yet*. Though it probably would in time. They did say that what America had one day England got the next.

When she was out of the shower and dry again she moved to a chest and opened the bottom drawer. From a small cardboard box she withdrew a long, rusty nail and a large, smooth stone. With these and the clay image she had no doubt of success. They'd be enough to kill Arthur ten times over.

That evening at art class she finished the clay model and carefully placed it in the small box she had brought with her for the purpose. As she did so the instructor, a tall woman with a face like a dispossessed spaniel, came to her, looked over her shoulder and said, 'All done, then, Mrs Armstrong?'

'Yes, all done.'

'I'm curious,' the instructor said, 'as to what you want it for . . .'

Doris turned to her and gave a bleak smile. 'Are you?' She put the lid on the box and sealed it with tape. Let the stupid woman be curious; she wasn't going to satisfy her curiosity. What was more, she wouldn't be coming back to the class after this evening; there'd be no need to.

That night as she lay awake in bed thinking of tomorrow and the festival she could hear Arthur's snoring through the wall. That was something else she wouldn't have to put up with for much longer. Just a little while and he'd never snore again.

The thirty-first. It had rained during the night but the morning was clear, bright and promising.

Over the breakfast table Arthur, as usual, was clearly unhappy about his eggs, and she watched, secretly pleased, as he pushed them to one side. 'Aren't you going to eat your eggs?' she said.

He frowned. 'You know I don't like them like this, Doris,' he said. 'I tell you every morning and next day they're just the same. Sometimes I think you just don't make the effort.'

She looked at him over her coffee cup, hating him. She was glad that his scrambled eggs were like rubber. Glad. If he'd been pleased with them she'd have been disappointed. And he was wrong to say that she didn't make the effort. She *did*. She had to have ways of showing her loathing for him and the eggs were one of those ways. 'I worked hard to prepare those eggs for you,' she said reproachfully.

After a few moments under her glare he pulled the plate back before him. 'I'll try to eat a little,' he murmured.

She watched then as he braced himself and dug a fork into the solid yellow mass. Added to his incompetence he had no guts, either. What a wimp. Any other man would have thrown the mess at the wall – which was what it deserved. Not Arthur, though; he put up with it. All the inedible food she had served up to him every morning for the past twenty years, and he accepted it all, ate it all. Her contempt for him grew.

When the evening came she went into her bedroom and took from the box the small clay figure. Then she put on her coat, took her door key and went quietly out of the room. A short ride down in the lift and a few minutes later she was leaving the foyer and stepping out into the late October evening. Moving to the garden behind the apartment block, she stepped over the grass to the ornamental pool where water cascaded into its centre from a little waterfall. She had always despised it so, this pathetic little attempt at re-creating nature; now she wouldn't have changed it for anything.

At the side of the pool she looked around, eyes glancing up

at the windows of the overlooking flats. She could see no one looking out at her. Then, carefully unwrapping the little clay figure, she stepped closer to the edge of the pool, leaned over and placed the figure on the lip of the waterfall. The water surging over the stone was icy cold. She pressed the figure firmly onto the stone, wedging it in. Then, satisfied that it was secure, she stepped back and looked at it. As she did so she thought of the words she had read in the book in the coven library: *Make ye a picture of clay, like unto the shape of thine enemy, and then, on the night of Samhain or Beltane place it in a running stream till it be worn away.* Well, it was in a running stream now – and it wasn't going to last long by the looks of things; already, even as she watched, the limbs were beginning to crumble . . .

Back upstairs she went straight to her room and began to get ready.

Well before nine o'clock she was dressed and eager to get away. Emerging from her room she came to a stop before the hall mirror and put down her bag – heavier this evening – and made a last survey of her appearance. She had taken great trouble with her makeup, and she had been to the hairdresser just that afternoon. She'd hardly eaten all day, either, and felt about as slim as she had felt in a long while. Under her floor-length deep-blue velvet cloak, her warm ceremonial robe fell to her ankles. Beneath it she wore nothing. She was ready. Now if only Arthur would hurry up, they could get going.

'Arthur?' she shouted in the direction of his bedroom. 'Come on, will you? We're going to be late.'

When he appeared a few minutes later she shook her head in exasperation. 'I thought you were getting ready,' she said.

'I *am* ready.'

'But – you've got your Burberry on.'

'I know.'

'You don't mean to say you're going in that, do you?'

'Why not? I shall take it off when we get there.'

'You'll take it off *now*. You can't go there looking like that. Where's your cloak? All the others will arrive in cloaks.'

'Oh, Doris, for Luci's sake – I can't stand that cloak. Every year I wear it, and I feel like an idiot.'

'Well, you'll look like an idiot in *that*. And how d'you think *I'm* going to feel? Of course that doesn't matter to you, does it? – showing me up. And stop blaspheming – I keep telling you!' She continued to glare at him. 'Well, I'm not going with you looking like that, so you can just go and put on your cloak.'

After a moment's hesitation he went away. When he came back a couple of minutes later Doris still wasn't happy. 'What's up with your cloak?' she asked, frowning. 'It's not hanging right. You look like a badly tied bag of laundry.'

He shrugged. 'Well – it's probably my underwear.'

'You're wearing *underwear?*'

'Two sets.'

'Tell me you're joking.'

'What's wrong? I shall be cold. It's not *that* warm, in case you hadn't noticed. I don't want to catch pneumonia.'

'You talk as if this were the Dark Ages. Haven't you ever heard of central heating? The Goldbergs' house will be very warm and comfortable. And we shan't be outside for more than a minute or so. For Hell's sake, go and take it off at once.'

'Oh, Doris, must I?'

'Of course you must. Oh, my Lord, what a picture! Everybody else dancing around in the total nude and you in your Fruit of the Loom Y-fronts. It makes me shudder to think of it.' She shook her head. 'You don't take any of this seriously, do you?'

'Satan Almighty, Doris,' he sighed, 'we go through this every year. If you want the truth, I'd much rather stay home tonight and watch TV.'

'Yes, that's all you're fit for. Look at you – a descendant of one of the greatest witches who ever lived and now, tonight of all nights, instead of wanting to go and celebrate our main festival you'd rather stay in and watch TV. And *stop blaspheming.*' She glared at him for a second, then turned, opened the door and strode toward the lift.

The Goldbergs, who were hosting the festival this year, were longtime members of the coven and lived in wide grounds in the heart of the countryside some miles west of Trowbridge. Arthur had wanted to drive but after experiencing a little difficulty getting the car out of the garage Doris had ordered him out of the driver's seat. 'My Lord, how can you be so *incompetent!*' she'd snapped as she got behind the wheel. They set off then and got there just after ten, and as Doris steered the Ford Capri along the drive she saw ahead of her a large number of other cars. A rough count gave a number somewhere above forty. She was pleased and her excitement took another surge.

She kept very close to the edge of the driveway as she pulled the car to a stop. A moment later Arthur opened the door, looked down and groaned. 'Can't you move it out a little, Doris? It's so muddy here; I'll mess up my shoes.'

Doris had known exactly what she was doing and she just shook her head and sighed a long-suffering sigh. 'Oh, Arthur, stop being such a damned wimp, will you.' She switched off the ignition, got out of the car and started off toward the front of the house. Arthur caught up with her just as she reached the front door where the porch was brightly illuminated by colourful lanterns.

The door was opened by Ralph Goldberg, dressed in a long robe with a gold-coloured sash tied loosely at the place where his waist used to be. He greeted them with smiles and words of welcome, at the same time raising his right hand above his head, thumb and pinky extended, in a salute to the devil. Doris repeated the gesture – as did Arthur in a halfhearted way – then they were taking off their outer garments and putting them into Ralph's arms. After that they moved through the hall into the main lounge where the rest of the party revelers were congregated.

'Shall we be sacrificing any chickens?' Steve Walker asked. 'I hope so. I've been looking forward to that.' He, Shirley

Goldberg and Doris were standing together in the centre of the crowd of chattering people with glasses of mulled wine in their hands. At his question Shirley shook her head.

'No, I'm afraid not. Ralph got the order in too late and there weren't any available. All they had left were dead ones – fresh or frozen. We could have got some live turkeys but I couldn't face the thought of being faced with eating turkey for days on end afterward. It's bad enough at Christmas when you have to keep up appearances.'

The party was well on and Doris was looking forward to the dance and then to being alone with Steve. She hadn't really had a chance to talk to him so far – not with Shirley Goldberg and other people milling around all the time. It wouldn't be long now, though, she thought. For the moment, however, Shirley was holding the reins and, in her customary name-dropping way, was holding the floor too – and was obviously out to impress.

'I got in touch with Joan last night,' she was saying.

'Joan?' Doris asked. 'Joan who?'

'Joan who? Joan of Arc, of course.'

'Oh, that Joan. How was she?'

'Still very bitter.'

'Well, it's understandable, isn't it?'

Shirley nodded. 'Very bitter. I told her – you ought to get some kind of counselling – or therapy. I mean, it's eating away at her. Though I suppose it's to be expected after what they did to her. Some people – they've got a lot to answer for.'

'Right.'

'Mind you, in many ways she only had herself to blame – and I as good as told her so. I mean, once you start admitting that you're hearing voices, then people are going to get your number pretty damn quick. Sure to. Still, she had a hard time, there's no denying, and it was rotten luck on her – being set up like that – being made to carry the can for the inefficiency of our armies. Still, she should have kept her mouth shut. If she'd done that, she could be alive today.'

'I suppose you're right.'

'Of course I'm right. There are procedures that have to be adhered to. You can't go yelling your mouth off and going about things in a half-assed way. You've got to do things *right* . . .'

Shirley's voice droned on while Doris repeated her words: *You've got to do things right. Right* – and that's how *she* was doing things.

Turning slightly, she saw Arthur sitting near the window in conversation with Thelma Winnecky, a young, blond widow from Purton. Then, glancing above Arthur's head, she saw through the window Ralph Goldberg on the lawn setting light to the bonfire. She looked at her watch. Eleven forty-five. The dancing would start very soon. She hadn't much time.

'Will you excuse me for a moment, please . . . ?' She smiled at Shirley – who was still in full flood – and briefly pressed Steve's hand. Then, turning, she moved from the room.

In the cloakroom near the front door she took from her bag the large, smooth, pale stone she had brought and, with her nail file, carefully scratched Arthur's name upon it. Then she put it back into the bag along with the nail, put on her cloak and went out into the hall, where she opened the front door and slipped out into the night.

Moving swiftly, she walked out onto the drive where the cars were parked. When she got to the Ford she stepped carefully over to the near-side door and, taking a small torch from her purse, shone its beam down at the spot where Arthur had stepped (so complainingly, the wimp!) onto the soft, muddy earth of the verge. And – yes! – very clearly the light picked out the shape of his footprints. Three of them, two right and one left – and as cleanly indented as if he'd worked at it. She smiled, reached back into her bag and took out the nail and the stone.

Holding the nail up against the dull light of the sky, she looked at it. It appeared to be just an ordinary, if rather old-fashioned, nail. It was *not* ordinary, though, and it had cost a bomb – not to mention the difficulty she'd had in getting hold of it. Well, it wasn't something you could get in the local supermarket or even in some fancy ironmonger's shop. What did you do – walk in and say, 'I'd like one coffin nail, please?' No, she'd had to go to some old hag of a witch in Frome and pay a fortune – in cash. Cash on the nail, so to speak.

Anyway, she'd got the nail – and it would be worth it, every penny. After a quick glance around she carefully placed the nail's point into the indented heel of Arthur's left footprint, then with the stone she hammered it into the ground. *On the night of Samhain take ye a naile from a coffin that has been buried in the earth,* the book had said, *and put it in the footprint of thy foe. Very soon thereafter thy foe shall sicken and perish.* The nail went in easily; the soil was quite soft. She straightened and looked down. No sign of it. She smiled, turned and moved away.

She didn't reenter the house straightaway but went round to the back where Ralph Goldberg was tending the fire and feeding it with wood. As he did so it crackled and blazed and shot out sparks and made swift moving shadows against the backcloth of the house. He looked around at her and smiled as she approached. 'Came out to get a breath of air, did you, Doris?' he asked.

She nodded, returning his smile. 'Yes – and to see how it's all going.'

'Oh, we'll be ready in a minute.' He threw on more wood. 'I want to get a good blaze going first. We don't want anyone to catch cold.'

'Right.' It was funny how things had changed over the years, she thought. Everyone was so comfort-conscious today. In the old days they'd have danced naked round the fire, either till the fire went out or till they dropped. Not now; now the actual dance around the fire was only a token thing – a quick dash naked out into the chill air, link hands and dance around the fire a couple of times and then back indoors to finish the celebrations in the warm.

Ralph glanced at his watch, adjusted a burning log on the

fire and gave a nod of satisfaction. 'I think we might as well start now.' He moved off toward the patio door, then paused briefly and looked back. 'Aren't you coming in to disrobe . . . ?'

'Yes, in a minute – I'll be right there.' As she spoke she put out her hands toward the heat of the flames and then turned to watch as he went on into the house.

As soon as he had gone she dipped her right hand into her bag and took out the stone. In the flickering light of the fire she looked at it. Arthur's name stood out clearly. (*Choose thy time with care, then take ye a stone, writ with the name of thine adversary . . .*) A quick glance toward the patio window and she took a step forward. (*. . . and place it in fire . . .*) She muttered a little prayer, took a breath and cast the stone into the heart of the flames.

And it was done. Everything was done. All she had to do now was wait. And she wouldn't have to wait very long. Within twelve hours of the hour of midnight Arthur would be dead.

She sat at the breakfast bar in the Goldbergs' kitchen drinking coffee. She had been there for a long time. There had been no sign of Arthur for a long while and she sat tense and expectant, waiting at any moment for someone to come in and say that he was dead, had been found lying dead in one of the Goldbergs' many spare bedrooms or on some sofa in some other part of the house. It looked as if he'd had a heart attack, they would say, and she would cry and try to look brave in the face of her great tragedy.

The thought should have cheered her more than it did. Oh, yes, she was glad, very glad, when she thought of Arthur getting out of her hair, out of her life at last, but when she thought of Steve Walker it was another matter. She'd seen hardly anything of him after their chat over cocktails and the dance around the fire. He had been close to her then as they'd all circled the crackling flames, and the grasp of his hand in hers had been firm and full of promise. But soon afterward he had just vanished. Then, later, wandering about the huge house alone, she had come upon two people in a room, lying together on a rug, limbs threshing, their movements accompanied by groans and sighs and muttered words. She'd backed out, but not before she had realized who the two were. One was Steve, she was sure. And the other? No mistaking that voice. Shirley Goldberg.

Later, while nursing a coffee, her disappointment and her anger, she'd put her robe back on; there didn't seem much point in doing otherwise. There was no one else around now – the others had all gone off long since to different rooms, either in pairs or groups of three, four, five or six. Now, sitting in the kitchen she turned at the sound of approaching footsteps and braced herself for the news. The door opened.

'Arthur . . .' She gaped at him.

He looked a little sheepish. ''Ah – there you are. I was wondering.'

Then her bitterness at the evening's disappointment flared up. 'Where the hell have you been?' she rapped out.

'Been? I haven't been anywhere.'

She shook her head in contempt and exasperation. 'Well – I want to go home. I've had enough.'

'But they'll be serving breakfast soon.'

'I don't want any breakfast. I just want to go home.' She waited, then when he didn't move she said, 'Didn't you hear me? I said I want to go home.'

He looked at her, sighed and nodded. 'Yes, dear. Whatever you say.'

They slipped away without saying their good-byes to anyone, and when they got outside she left Arthur for a moment, went round to the back of the house and looked at the remains of the bonfire. Now it was just a pile of cold ashes. Poking into it with a stick, she uncovered the stone she had put there last night. Bending, she picked it up, blew off the dust and looked at it closely. And suddenly she felt a little touch of pleasure in the midst of her frustration and dissatisfaction.

On the stone there was not a sign of Arthur's name. (*If the fire shall destroy the name then so shall the owner of that name be destroyed . . .*) The name had been burned clean away. With a little smile she dropped the stone back into the ashes and went to join Arthur where he sat waiting in the car.

When they got back to Stratton she put the car away while Arthur went on upstairs. She didn't follow him immediately, but first went toward the communal garden in the centre of which lay the ornamental pool and the little waterfall. When she reached the pool she looked at the lip of the stone over which the water ran and saw that there was no trace left of the clay figure. It was gone, without trace. The water had completely worn it away.

And all at once the depression that had hung over her since Steve's betrayal was lifted. What did it matter, anyway? He meant nothing to her. And there were plenty of other men in the world. And soon, very soon, with Arthur gone, she would be free to play the field. She looked at her watch. Just after six. There was very little time to go now. It could happen at any moment. She turned and looked up toward the windows of the flat. 'Arthur,' she whispered, 'your hours are numbered.'

Upstairs in the flat she pushed open his bedroom door and found him getting ready for bed. He turned to her and gave a little shrug. 'I thought I'd just have a nap for a while . . .'

Hiding the elation that was growing within her, she took in the look of exhaustion on his face and said, 'Don't you want any breakfast?' After all, she said to herself, every condemned man was entitled to a good breakfast.

He shook his head. 'No, thanks. I'm feeling very tired. I'm too old for all those goings-on. Staying up all night, cavorting around. I think I'll give it a miss next year.'

You certainly will, Doris thought, then aloud she said, 'Didn't you get any sleep at the Goldbergs'? There were enough beds.'

'Oh, I dozed a bit,' he said. 'But nothing much.' He climbed into bed and pulled the covers up over him. 'But I think I'll sleep now all right.'

She stayed there in the room until he was settled and then crept out into the hall. After a while she began to move around the flat doing odd little chores – for no other reason than simply to keep herself occupied. Then after a while she crept to his bedroom, silently pushed open the door and looked in. The curtains were drawn against the light, but in the gloom she could hear the sound of his breathing. The suspense was unbearable. When was it going to happen?

Later, just before eleven, she quietly went back into his room and in the half-light stood listening to the sound of his breathing. It sounded strange: slow and faint, with touches of harshness as if the breaths came with difficulty. She moved closer to the bed and looked down at him. His flesh had a grayish look about it – a dead look. She called his name but he made no response. Carefully she reached in beneath the bed cover, located his wrist and felt his pulse. Sweet Lord, it was only just discernible – only the faintest little flutter there.

Letting him go, she stepped back from the bed. Now all she had to do was wait. Smiling, she turned and left the room.

Taking the morning paper into the sitting room, she settled in her favourite chair. It was impossible to concentrate, though, and in the end she just gave in to the warm, sparkling thoughts that crowded her mind and, closing her eyes, she laid back her head and let the thoughts take over.

A sudden sound brought her head toward the door, and she realized that she had been sleeping.

Arthur was standing there in his dressing gown. He smiled at her. 'You should have gone to bed and had a real nap, like I did,' he said. 'You look as if you could do with it.'

She gaped at him, speechless. When she had found her voice she said, 'How do you feel?'

He nodded, smiling. 'Oh, much better now after my rest.'

'That's good,' she murmured. 'You look better.'

She gazed at him, realizing that her words were true – he *did* look better. So much better. For one thing his colour was better than it had been for years – and also he seemed to be holding himself so much straighter – and she saw too an unaccustomed suppleness in his movement as he turned, stepped toward the window, opened it and breathed in the fresh air.

'Now,' he said, turning to smile back at her, 'I could really eat some breakfast.'

She nodded and, almost in a daze, got up and started off toward the kitchen, Arthur walking behind her. 'I've already mixed the eggs,' he said. 'I just have to finish them off.'

'No, *I'll* do it,' she retorted quickly.

'I really don't mind, Doris. Honestly.'

She had reached the kitchen table now and she turned back to face him. She had never hated him so much. Scathingly she said, '*You'll* do it, Arthur? *You?*' She laughed. 'Dear Hell, the most inefficient, incompetent man this side of the English Channel. I should let *you* loose in my kitchen? That'll be the day.'

Ten minutes later she moved to the breakfast table, where she placed before him a plate of scrambled eggs. Then, setting down in her own place the two lightly boiled eggs she had prepared so perfectly, she sat and began to eat.

As she ate – without looking at him – she waited for him to complain. There was silence, though, and at last she lifted her head and gazed at him. He sat there, very still, just looking down at his plate. And, dear Satan, he looked better than he had for ages. Nothing had worked – not the clay image, nor the coffin nail nor the stone. But how could it be? She had done everything exactly according to the book. Or at least she had tried to. Then what had gone wrong? Was it that the name on the stone hadn't quite disappeared in the fire? Was it that the nail she had bought hadn't come from a coffin? Was it that the clay model hadn't been quite faithful enough in its likeness? Or was it perhaps because there had been no live chickens at the festival and therefore no blood had been spilled . . . ? The questions went on churning through her mind. Whatever had happened, though, it hadn't worked. He was still here.

Thrusting the thoughts, the questions from her mind, she waited for him to speak, to say something about the eggs. Yet still he said nothing. That wasn't like him; and this time she had truly excelled herself; there was no way that anyone could eat the food she had put before him. Every bit of her seething hatred and frustration had gone into its preparation. He had to react soon.

And then, as she watched him he gave a little sigh, pushed the empty plate away from him, got up from the table and moved toward the kitchen. 'What's the matter?' she called after him. 'You feel sick?'

When he came back a few seconds later she turned to him as he approached. He had a weird, calm look about him that she had never seen before. And suddenly she was afraid. 'Arthur,' she said, 'don't look at me like that.'

'I've told you, Doris,' he said, shaking his head, 'I've told you over and over again – I don't like my eggs like that.'

Calmly, he raised the hatchet in his right hand and brought it down. Very efficiently, more than competently, and without an ounce of wasted effort, he split her skull from crown to jaw with one clean downward blow. Then, aiming the ax from the side, he struck a second time and severed her head from her neck.

Later, when he had cleaned up the mess, he beat up more eggs and scrambled them the way he liked.

PEACE OFFERING

GREG got to the station a good while before the train was due, and for the next twenty-five minutes kicked his cold heels on the dreary platform. But he didn't mind the wait.

Eventually the train drew in and he climbed aboard. Later, when he reached London, he dismissed the idea of a tube or a bus – though he knew the route perfectly well – and instead flagged down a taxi. Giving the address to the driver, he settled back in the comfortable seat, stretching his legs before him.

He tried to relax, but found it was utterly impossible. How could he relax? How could he – today of all days? This grey, miserable-looking, snow-bound day was one of the happiest – and certainly one of the most important – days of his whole life.

Lighting a cigarette he mentally urged the taxi to move faster, muttering soft, impatient oaths at any of the other vehicles that momentarily impeded his own progress. He wanted to be there now – *now*, without delay. The sooner he got there, the sooner they could both leave.

After the longest forty-five minutes he had ever known, he was at last deposited outside the dingy house in the shabby, dilapidated East London Street. He paid the driver – adding a larger tip than was necessary – then turned and, with a firm, light tread, strode up the short path to the front door. Reaching for the bell with Maureen's name, he pressed it. Waiting for her to answer, he found himself suddenly aware of his own heartbeat; it was due partly to his excitement at the thought of having Jeannie back, he realised, and, partly due to a slight feeling of anxiety at the prospect of meeting Maureen again. But it had to be got through, and besides, it wouldn't take long. He rang the bell again. He knew she was in; she was expecting him. His ungloved hand holding the box of chocolates was cold; his breath vaporous on the December air.

And then Maureen was at the door.

She stood there smiling at him across the threshold, her smile a little forced, perhaps, a trifle nervous, but nevertheless a smile. At once Greg felt a fraction more secure, felt a little of the tension start to drain away. Thank God, he thought, she's not going to create a scene.

'Come in.' Maureen stepped aside and he moved into the small, dismal hallway. He waited while she closed the front door and went past him, then followed her up the two flights of stairs and into the top-floor flat that she had acquired since their separation.

'Give me your coat . . .'

He took off his overcoat and handed it to her, and she went from him and hung it on a peg in the hall. When she came back he gave her the chocolates.

'Well – thank you.' Drawing the box from inside the paper bag she looked at the well-known design on the lid. 'My favourites, too. You remembered. But you shouldn't have – really.'

Greg shrugged away her thanks. The chocolates had been the result of a last-minute whim that had come to him while he was buying his cigarettes. Now he was glad; she seemed pleased with the gift.

Still looking at the box of chocolates, Maureen said with a little laugh:

'Beware geeks when they come bearing gifts, right?'

At her words Greg felt his own smile slip a little, and said quickly, 'Oh, no, please, Maureen, don't say that.'

'I'm only joking,' she said. 'It's very sweet of you.' She paused, then added, 'A token?'

He shrugged, awkwardly. 'Sort of, I suppose.'

She was silent for a moment, then, 'Good,' she said, ' – I accept.'

She turned away and he followed her trim, blue-clad figure

into the small lounge, with its even smaller dining recess off to the left. He looked around and saw at once that they were alone. He was about to ask, 'Where is – ?' but stopped himself, deciding that there would be time enough for such questions a little later. It was best not to appear too eager. With an attempt at casualness he sat down in the chair Maureen indicated, then looked up at her as she stood with her head bent over the chocolate box. Her blonde hair fell forward on either side of her face, momentarily masking her features. Jeannie's hair was the same colour and texture. He listened for some noise, some sign of Jeannie, but the only sound was the crinkling of the cellophane wrapping as Maureen removed it from the chocolate box. 'Lovely,' she said, smiling. 'We'll have some after lunch.'

'After lunch?' he said. 'Oh – oh, I didn't know you were expecting me to stay on for lunch.'

As he spoke he was aware that his eagerness to be away again was transparently clear in his voice and face. And quickly he admonished himself, telling himself to make an effort, to relax and let things take their course. After all, he reasoned, the whole thing was far more difficult for her than it was for him.

'Don't you *want* to stay for lunch?' Maureen said, having picked up the note of dismay in his tone. 'I should think it's the least you could do.'

'Yes,' he said. 'Yes, of course – that would be – be very nice. It's just that I   I wasn't expecting it.' He was aware that his words sounded stiff and awkward, and to cover the moment he took out his cigarettes and offered her one – and then remembered that she had stopped smoking.

'Have you forgotten so soon?' Maureen said.

She moved away from him then into the kitchen, and he put the cigarettes back in his pocket and followed her. Standing in the doorway, he watched as she expertly chopped and prepared the various vegetables. After carefully adding salt to a pan of carrots, she turned to him, smiling.

'You're dying to know when Jeannie's getting back, aren't you?' she said. 'Well, why don't you ask, you big silly?'

But then before he could reply, she went on:

'Mother's here for a few days. I asked her to come down. I felt I – I needed somebody at this time.'

He nodded while he inwardly groaned. He didn't look forward to spending any time in the company of Maureen's mother. He and Mrs Cavendish had never seen eye to eye. From the early days of their marriage she had made it clear how much she resented him. And he had never been able to get through that resentment. But she would feel that way about anyone, he reflected. It just so happened that he was the one who had dared break into the almost unnaturally close relationship that existed between the woman and her daughter.

He saw that Maureen was crying. Quite suddenly she was crying. He took a step towards her, but managed to resist the impulse to reach out, to soothe, to offer comfort.

'It's not fair,' she said in a broken, little-girl's voice. 'It's just not fair.'

'Maureen, please don't . . .' He knew it was probably better that he should say nothing, but it was impossible just to stand there.

'Oh, it's all right for you,' she said. '*You won.*' She glared at him for a few seconds, then, with a dismissive shrug, swung back to her pots and pans.

When a little time had gone by he said, 'Jeannie will have enjoyed having your mother here as well.' And then, casually he asked: 'Where did they go?'

Maureen reached out for the oven-cloth. Her eyes were dry now, he noticed, thankfully. She even managed something of a smile as she spoke.

'Well, you know Mum – always a fresh air fanatic. I think she mentioned something about the park.'

'On a day like *this*?' he said. He was about to add, *You know how Jeannie feels the cold*, but stopped himself in time.

'Oh, stop worrying, for God's sake,' Maureen said sharply. 'She's well wrapped up. She's warm enough.'

'Yes, of course. I'm sure she is . . .' He was anxious to avoid any dissension, no matter how trivial it might be. He watched as she opened the oven door to check on the roast. Her face was set.

'How long will they be?' he asked.

'Not long now. They'll be here for lunch. I told Mum to be sure not to be late. Anyway,' she added, 'when there's food on the table you can bet Jeannie won't be far away.'

Inwardly Greg sighed. He felt sure that Maureen had purposely allowed Jeannie to go out to the park – to be away from the flat when he arrived. It was probably her way of making him suffer. 'It's just that – that I expected her to be here,' he said.

'*Oh, dear,*' Maureen said witheringly, 'I've inconvenienced you – so sorry about that.' She shook her head. 'Listen,' she added bitterly, 'you've already got *everything*, and you stand there complaining because your schedule's at risk of being put out a bit. What's the matter with you? What more do you want?'

'Maureen, please –' he began, but she went on, undeterred:

'She's *yours*. *Yours*. Legally. I've lost all rights – all claim to her – *thanks to you*. You made sure of that.'

With her words the ugly scenes in the courtroom came back to him. He forced the pictures aside as she continued:

'Yes, and I've got *nothing* now. *Nothing*. But that's all you're entitled to expect when some stupid, doddering old bastard decides that you're not a fit mother!' She slammed down the oven-cloth amongst the meat and vegetable trimmings, her voice growing louder in her anger. 'What right had they to sit in judgment of me?'

Greg kept silent, while through his mind flashed a series of memories, all having in common instances of Maureen's behaviour during their few years together – her violence towards him, her capriciousness, her quiet rages when she

failed to get her way. Even now the memories had the power
to shake his equilibrium. All were best left undisturbed – like
the courtroom scenes – which were much too recent and too
raw.

Cutting into his thoughts, Maureen went on with her tirade
of blame and resentment. 'And now,' she said through tight,
grim lips, 'I'm told I can only see my daughter once a month.'

Greg, saying nothing, lowered his glance, unable to face the
hostility and hatred in her eyes. But she was not to be halted.

'Once a month,' she said. 'Twelve visits a year. And for just
two days at a time. And then only with the visits supervised.
Who would believe it? A mother never allowed to be alone
with her own daughter. Nice, eh? And whose doing was *that*,
eh?' She was glaring at him. 'And you – look at you – standing
there as cool as you like. You give her up to me for just a couple
of days, then take her away again – for another month. And
you've got the nerve to go whining just because she's not on
the doorstep to greet you with open arms!'

There was a cold, charged silence, then Greg said, 'Maureen
– let's not do this. I know it's hard for you. And I do understand
how you feel. I do – believe me. And you must know that I
didn't want it to come to this. But I had no choice. We couldn't
have gone on as we were – none of us . . .'

She stared at him for a moment or two longer, then, seem-
ing almost to sag slightly, she said,

'Ah, what does it matter now, anyway? It's too late to change
anything now.'

He said nothing to this. There was nothing to say. He
couldn't keep up with her mercurial moods, that much was
certain; but then, he had never been able to. There had been
so many times during their marriage when she had appeared
almost as a stranger to him.

With an effort to bring the situation onto calmer ground,
he said lightly, gesturing to the pots and pans on the stove:
'You know, you shouldn't have done all this – gone to all this
trouble. And it looks as if you've got enough for an army.'

'Mum helped me,' she said. 'Anyway, you always have a good appetite – like Jeannie. After a cold, bracing hour in the park she'd come back ravenous – remember?' The flicker of a smile suddenly appeared on her face. 'Listen, you go and sit down. Let me get on.'

'Is there anything I can do?'

'No, you go and sit down and relax.'

Greg moved back into the lounge, sat down in an easy chair, picked up a newspaper and began to glance through it. As he did so Maureen bustled back and forth setting the dining table. Greg took in almost nothing of what he was trying to read, conscious always of the tension in the place. And the worst part was yet to come, he knew. This was the first of Jeannie's visits to her mother since the ruling, and he dreaded the moment when he would be leaving the house with her. Still, he told himself, he'd face that moment when it arrived.

After a time he put the paper aside, got up and looked in on the kitchen again. Maureen was mixing gravy, and he watched her as she tasted it, eyes screwed up in anticipation of the heat, the wooden spoon held fastidiously in her small, capable hand. She nodded, satisfied.

'I think we're about ready here,' she said. 'If you'd like to go sit at the table we can eat.'

'But the others aren't here yet.'

Maureen consulted the kitchen clock. 'They ought to be here by now,' she said, frowning. 'I told Mum not later than one.'

Greg went over to the window and looked down onto the snow-bound street below. There was no sign of his ex-mother-in-law or of his two-year-old daughter. It really was too bad of Mrs Cavendish to stay out so long, he thought. She knew that he would be anxious to get away, to get home.

Home. Home was the little house just on the outskirts of Salisbury in Wiltshire. Greg thought of the decorating he had lately been doing there – of Jeannie's room – the care and the love he had lavished on it. And it was finished now. In Jeannie's absence he got the rest of it done, added the finishing touches. He could hardly wait for her to see it, to see the look on her round, baby-face when she saw it all – the pink linen flowers he had pasted on the walls, the pink curtains, the pink bedspread. Pink, everything pink – the exact same shade as the ribbons that she loved to wear in her hair.

And there was Julia too. Julia, his new wife. Julia whom Maureen, of course, never ever mentioned. For that was another bone of contention and bitterness – that Jeannie was daily coming to love Julia with all her heart.

As he moved away from the window, Maureen entered carrying dishes of vegetables which she set down on the cork mats. 'This is the last time Jeannie will be at lunch with Mum and me, so I want it to be special,' she said. She waved a hand towards the table. 'Please – sit down.'

Greg took a seat in the corner of the recess, and a moment later his heart leapt with joy as he heard the sound of footsteps on the stairs. He was about to rise but then decided to stay where he was; he'd surprise Jeannie.

But to his surprise a dog came bounding in. Greg didn't know they'd kept a dog. The animal, a black labrador, sought him out immediately, thrusting a wet, cold nose against his hand and his thigh. Greg shifted his leg irritably, at the same time straining his ears for the sound of Jeannie's voice, but he could hear nothing above the raucous voice of his ex-mother-in-law as she talked animatedly to Maureen in the kitchen. Why, he wondered, didn't someone tell Jeannie that he was here, waiting for her . . . ?

Sitting hidden from the main lounge and from the kitchen, he sorted out the noises that came through to him, listening to the scrape of feet on the linoleum, the slam of the bathroom door. Then Maureen appeared again. Taking in the look on his face, she said with a sigh:

'You can relax now. She's here.' Depositing the tray on the table she called over her shoulder in the direction of the bathroom, 'Come on now. We're ready. We're waiting for you.'

As she set down the dishes of vegetables, Greg realised that in spite of his impatience to get moving, he was hungry.

'Oh, it's *you*.'

Greg looked around to see Mrs Cavendish looking coldly at him as she approached the table.

'Hello.' He tried a smile, but it didn't quite work. 'Were you expecting somebody else?' he said.

Maureen said to her mother, 'You should have seen him, Mum. Like a cat on hot bricks. Just couldn't wait for his darling little girl to get back.'

The older woman sniffed. She had a hard, deeply seamed face. Her eyes were the same colour blue as Maureen's. Greg saw them flash as she looked towards him – a quick, hate-filled glance. 'Typical,' she said.

'He brought me chocolates,' Maureen said. 'A peace-offering of sorts, I believe.'

'Oh, him and his peace-offerings,' Mrs Cavendish said. 'Did you accept them?'

'Yes, of course I did.' Maureen sneered across the table at Greg who sat there hot with embarrassment. 'Of course I took his chocolates. And he agreed to accept my peace-offering in return.' She turned to Greg then, addressing her next words to him. 'Perhaps then there'll be an end to it.'

Greg said into the sudden silence: 'There are only three place settings.'

Maureen began to laugh, and Mrs Cavendish joined in and they sat there rocking. Then Mrs Cavendish mimicked him, sneering:

'*There are only three place settings*. Huh, typical.'

Maureen pushed the meat tray towards him. 'You can be man of the house for the last time,' she said. 'We'll let you do the carving.'

Greg found himself taking up the fork and carving knife. 'Where's Jeannie?' he asked.

'*Where's Jeannie?*' Mrs Cavendish mimicked again, then, turning to Maureen, she said, 'Oh, go on, Maureen. He'll never be satisfied. We'll never get any peace.'

'I told you she'd be here,' Maureen said, sighing, leaning over the table. With a cool, graceful movement she lifted the domed cover of the huge meat dish. 'You see? Pink ribbons and all, look.'

And there was Jeannie. As Greg stared aghast at the dreadful thing before him, Mrs Cavendish said, smiling:

'Just look at him, Maureen. He looks as if he's lost fifty pence and found five.'

TRAVELLING LIGHT

'**B**ut you said you'd be arriving *tomorrow* . . .'

The little woman behind the reception desk looked more and more flustered and bewildered. Gideon turned to the tall stranger who stood nearby, shrugged helplessly, then turned back to the woman. She was looking at him anxiously through her thick-lensed spectacles.

'No,' Gideon said patiently, ' – I wrote to say that I would be getting here *today*. My *wife* would be arriving *tomorrow*, I said. But I'd be here *today*. I *told* you. I thought I'd made it perfectly clear . . .' His voice trailed off in the face of her helpless, wide-eyed inadequacy.

'I'm so sorry,' she murmured. She seemed almost on the point of tears. 'I really am very sorry. I don't know how there came to be such a mix-up.' She shook her head. 'And there's nothing at all available for tonight . . .'

'But what am I supposed to do?' Gideon said. 'It's late. How do I find something else at this time of night?'

'I'm so sorry,' the woman said.

As she spoke these words the tall stranger took a step forward, opening his mouth to speak. At once the woman, obviously recognizing him as a former guest, forestalled him.

'Oh, we've got *your* room, Mr Travers,' she said. 'Don't worry about that.'

The man nodded and murmured his thanks. The woman went on:

'Though it looks as if they've given you a double room, a twin instead of the single you booked . . .' Weakly, she smiled away the inefficiency. 'Of course, though, you won't be charged the full rate.'

During this brief exchange Gideon, irritated and annoyed

at the inefficiency and inconvenience, stooped to pick up his suitcases. Now he'd have to start searching other hotels in the area. It was a bloody nuisance.

And then the stranger, Travers, spoke.

'My room,' he said, turning to the woman behind the desk, ' – the double you've given me – it does have two beds in it, yes?' He spoke with a strong Scottish accent. 'If so, maybe we can work something out.' He turned, smiling towards Gideon. 'I really don't like the thought of this poor gentleman having to search the town at this time of night looking for somewhere to sleep.'

As his suggestion hung in the air, the woman looked from him to Gideon.

'Sir,' Travers said to Gideon, 'you'd be most welcome to share my room. After all, it's only for a night – and *I* certainly don't mind.'

'Well – ' Gideon said, 'that is really most kind of you. Are you sure it wouldn't be putting you out?'

'Not at all. Not in the least. I'd be glad to help.'

A feeling of relief swept over Gideon. He beamed at the older man. 'Well – if you're quite sure.'

'Perfectly.' Travers gave him a gap-toothed smile. 'As I said, I'm only too glad to help.'

A little while later, up in the room, Gideon sat on the edge of his bed clipping his fingernails and waiting for Travers to finish in the bathroom. Carefully he placed the nail-parings in a nearby ashtray. Already, from the bedside table Carole smiled out at him from the narrow leather frame of her photograph. Tomorrow, Gideon thought. Tomorrow . . .

Travers had left the bathroom door open, and now, as Gideon turned, he could see the other man as he stood at the wash-basin, a towel about his naked waist. He was shaving with an old-fashioned, open, cut-throat razor. Gideon watched, admiring the dexterity with which he handled the cruel-looking instrument.

'I never before saw anyone use one of those,' Gideon said, ' – not outside those old Mafia movies anyway.'

'Oh, you can't beat it,' Travers said, smiling. Neatly he skimmed the blade over his prominent Adam's apple. 'It does the best job. By far.'

Gideon said, grimacing: 'Seeing you doing that makes me think of those terrible murders that have been going on. The papers are full of them.'

'Oh, yes, those terrible wife-slayings,' Travers said. 'Yes, very strange business.'

'Just ghastly,' Gideon said. 'Seven killings – all practically identical in pattern. All carried out in full view of reliable witnesses, and in each case by the victim's husband.' He shuddered. 'It's like some awful disease. Imagine – seven of them.'

'You're wrong,' Travers said. 'There've been eight. There was another one last night. I heard it on the news.' He carefully circumnavigated a large wart on his chin. 'Just like all the others. Her throat cut from ear to ear. Head almost severed from the body. Took place in the street this time. In Brighton. Husband arrested again. There were plenty of witnesses. As usual.'

Gideon continued to watch as, with sensitive fingers, Travers tested the smoothness of his jaw. The man was not a particularly attractive specimen, Gideon thought. His skin was unusually pallid. It had a wan, preserved look about it, as if it was rarely exposed to the sun. Over the pale flesh of his chest grew a mat of short, spiky hair – like his eyebrows, eyelashes and the hair on his head, all of a light, sandy redness.

All at once, becoming aware of Travers's eyes upon him, Gideon, embarrassed, looked away.

'So your wife's joining you tomorrow,' Travers said.

'Yes.' Gideon nodded happily. He and Carole had been apart for three months now, and these last days had sometimes seemed never-ending. 'We've had to be apart for a while,' he said. 'I've been doing this course up in the north. It's not over yet, but at least we thought we could spend my holiday together – in a nice place.'

'I guess you've been missing her pretty badly.'

'Oh, yes,' Gideon said, ' – so much. I can't wait for her to get here.' He thought of Carole, pictured her soft features, her bright, clear blue eyes. Marrying her had been the best thing he had ever done. All pride, he shrugged, smiled. 'She's . . . just great . . .'

'That's good to hear,' Travers said. 'A happy couple – it's very nice to hear.' He shook his razor dry and slipped it back into its case. 'Save me shaving in the morning,' he said. 'I'm not so fussy.' He put the razor-case into a plastic toilet bag. 'You people who go around with loads of suitcases – I believe in travelling light.' He came to the doorway. 'You want to come in here?'

'Yes – thanks.' Gideon rose from the bed. 'I think I'll take a shower.'

With the bathroom door closed behind him, Gideon stripped and stood before the mirror. Unlike Travers, he had a handsome body, tanned golden brown by the sun. His hair grew thick and black, its darkness contrasting with the whiteness of his smile. And today he had a real reason to smile: tomorrow he would be seeing Carole again.

When he emerged from the bathroom a while later he found Travers lying back smoking a cigarette.

Gideon lay down on his own bed, his towelling robe around him. 'God, I'm tired,' he said. 'All that travelling. I think I'll sleep for a while.'

'What time are you expecting your wife to arrive?' Travers asked. He had picked up and was studying the photograph of Carole. 'Early?'

'About ten o'clock,' Gideon said. Somehow he resented Travers handling the picture. He watched him anxiously.

'She's very pretty,' Travers said.

'Yes . . .'

'You meeting her at the station?'

'No. Here. Down in the foyer. She wasn't sure which train she'd manage, so . . .' He paused. 'I'll just wait downstairs for her. It was her idea.'

With a little sense of relief he watched as Travers replaced the photograph on the bedside table. He gave a yawn, and Travers nodded, and said,

'You do look a little tired. You should take a nap maybe.'

'Yes, I am,' Gideon said. 'The travelling – like I said. That always does it for me.' He yawned again, then lay back and, smiling in his relaxation, stretched out full-length on the bed. Minutes later he was asleep.

When Travers leaned over him to clip from his head a small lock of hair, Gideon almost awoke. For a moment he stirred uneasily, a frown briefly creasing the smoothness of his tanned brow. His mouth opened slightly in a silent, unknowing pro-test, and then he sank again, back into his slumber. Travers, standing above him, held the lock of hair in his hand for a moment, then added it to the little collection of nail-parings he had taken out of the ashtray. He smiled. Yes. It would be quite enough. It would be perfect.

In the morning, when Gideon awoke, he saw that Travers was still asleep. In the dim light the shape of him was just visible as he lay bundled up under the bed-covers.

Moving into the bathroom, Gideon turned on the water to shave. He felt a little odd and not quite his usual self, almost as if he was suffering from a hangover. But that couldn't be – he'd had nothing to drink last night.

The hot water gushed from the tap, clouding the glass. Yawning, Gideon switched on the light and rubbed a clear circle on the glass. And then his heart turned over.

In the glass he looked in horror at his white skin and the short, sandy-red hair that grew on his head and chest. He opened his mouth in a short, silent cry of fear and saw that two of his front teeth were missing. The hand that leapt to his face felt the ugly wart that stood out on his chin. It couldn't be.

How could it be? Gasping for breath, he leaned over the basin, clutching at the rim for support.

Minutes passed, and eventually he straightened, looked into the glass again and saw, as before, Travers's reflection. It could not be possible. It could not.

Breath trembling in his throat, he turned to the door and opened it. From the bedroom before him came the sounds of Travers stirring as he got up from his bed. Gideon watched as he pushed aside the covers and got to his feet.

Through sandy-coloured eyelashes Gideon took in the man's dark, waving hair, his smooth, tanned cheek – the cheek that Carole had so often kissed. Aware of Gideon's eyes upon him, Travers smiled at him, showing white, even teeth.

'Don't look like that,' he said. 'It won't be for long.' And the voice was Gideon's own voice.

Standing in the bathroom doorway, Gideon continued to stare, uncomprehending, eyes wide with horror. After a moment Travers said, with a note of impatience:

'You're not going to stand there all day, are you? I need to use the bathroom.'

'Oh God,' Gideon said – and spoke his horror-stricken words with a Scottish accent. 'Oh God, oh God, oh God, oh God . . .'

Travers smiled again, his cheek dimpling in the way that Carole had always loved. 'Come on,' he said, ' – the time's getting on, and I've got an appointment at ten.'

With his words he stepped towards the bathroom, and Gideon dumbly moved aside to allow him to enter. And then he stood there, open-mouthed, as Travers opened his toilet bag and took from it the razor-case.

Lifting out the razor, Travers tested it on his thumb, carefully trying the keenness of its shining blade.

'That's it,' he said. 'Perfect. Now – I must get dressed. I've got to meet a pretty lady downstairs. Down in the foyer.' He turned to Gideon and gave him a grotesque, conspiratorial wink. 'She'll be expecting me to be there, and I mustn't keep her waiting.'

MOMMY'S PROGRAMME

'OH, for God's sake, Laurie, will you hurry up!'
Sarah Rooney shifted the shopping bags more securely into the crook of her arm and snatched roughly at the hand of her three-year-old daughter.

'But the kittens,' Laurie protested. 'You said we could stop to look in the window. You said we'd go by the pet store. You promised.'

'Well, there just isn't the time. Next time. It'll have to be next time.'

'But you promised.' A whine crept into Laurie's voice and Sarah released the hand to slap at it wildly in her anger and impatience.

'The TV repairman's coming round to fix the set,' she snapped. 'We've gotta get back for when he arrives. I told him four o'clock so we must be there. I've got to get it fixed before my soap. I can't miss that.'

'Oh, that silly old TV,' Laurie pouted. 'That silly old programme.'

At this, Sarah slapped her again, but harder this time so that Laurie began to cry in a tiresome, peevish way.

'Oh, shut up!' Sarah felt hot, sticky and irritable. The store had been so overcrowded and they'd had to wait ages at the check-out. And it would be today, of course, just when she was anxious to get back to the house. 'And hurry up!' she added, yanking at the small hand clutched in her own. 'You're just like your father was. You'd be glad if I never got any fun at all!'

Opening the car door she dumped the bags of groceries onto the back seat. Laurie carried a smaller bag and Sarah grabbed at it unceremoniously and placed it along with the others. She turned to the child.

'Well, get in. Get in. Don't just stand there. Dummy.'

As they drove out of the parking lot she took a quick glance at her watch. With luck they would just make it in time. She pressed her foot down harder on the accelerator, pulled out swiftly, precariously in front of an oncoming Pontiac, over-took – with inches to spare – a pale blue Ford, and sped off along the highway. They'd make it; she was determined.

Scraping through on the tail-end of an amber light Laurie clutched at her mother's arm. 'Oh, Mommy, don't drive so fast. Please. It's scary. You're driving too fast.'

Sarah didn't answer, but shook off the hand. She was concentrating on the busy road and the intersection up ahead. Laurie spoke again.

'Mommy, don't! I don't like it when you drive too fast!'

'Shut up! Will you shut up.' Sarah felt that her nerves might snap. The traffic, Laurie's constant whining, the time, the seconds ticking away – it was all too much to cope with, she thought. With an effort she forced herself to remain calm, and consciously she softened her tone. 'Don't worry, baby. You'll be okay. Mommy knows just what she's doing.' Her tone was desperately sweet. 'You just be a good girl. We'll soon be home.'

Reaching the junction, Sarah turned the wheel to the right. Not far to go now. She said brightly, smiling, 'I bought ice cream. Your favourite. Peach. How about that? When we get in you can have peach ice cream. Doesn't that sound good?'

Laurie nodded, smiling. 'Can I have raspberry syrup on it too, please? Oh, Mommy, can I?'

'Yes, sweetie, if you like.'

'You promise?'

'I promise. That'll be real nice. Right?'

'Oh, yes!'

'I'll tell you what, honey. When we get back you can get us both a dish of ice cream with raspberry syrup, and we can eat while we watch the TV, huh? Doesn't that sound yummy?'

Turning onto Camden Avenue, Sarah peered ahead for

a sight of the TV repairman. She couldn't have missed him. They had to be in time.

Yes, there was his van. And there he was, just about to get in.

Foot harder still on the accelerator, Sarah punched the horn – a long, ear-splitting blast, then watched, unbelievably relieved as the man stopped and looked towards her car. She waved to him and he waved back in acknowledgement and stood there waiting. With rubber protesting on the road surface she brought the car to a screeching halt.

'Oh, my *God*!' Dramatically clutching her ample breast she heaved her bulk from the driver's seat. Gasping, she confronted the young man. 'I thought we'd never get here in time!' She sounded breathless, and the sweat of her exertion and anxiety showed clearly beneath her armpit, darkening the blue of her tight-fitting dress. She ran a hand, distraught, through her bleached, faded hair. 'You can't imagine the trouble I've had getting back,' she said. 'That goddamn store! It's just impossible.'

'Looks like it's your lucky day,' the man said. 'You made it just in time.' He looked Italian, she vaguely thought. Good-looking, but a bit on the lean side.

'Good. Come on.' Snatching the keys from the ignition, she slammed the door shut. From inside the car Laurie cried out in momentary panic and alarm.

'Mommy! Mommy!'

'Oh, my God!' Sarah grinned at the young man. 'I'm forgetting my own kid! I don't know what I'm doing anymore!' She laughed raucously. 'Okay, baby, out you come.'

When Laurie was outside Sarah turned back to the man. 'Let's get you started first, then I'll come back for my groceries.'

She led the way up the garden path and into the house. In the lounge the man set down his tool box and switched on the TV set. 'What's the trouble exactly?' he asked.

'The darn picture's so bad.' Sarah demonstrated with her

hands. 'It seems to shake all the time. It's hopeless.' She waited until the faulty image appeared then pointed, saying, 'There! You see what I mean?'

The man adjusted the position of the set and began to work with a screwdriver. Near his shoulder Sarah hovered, her anxiety showing now in small distracted movements of her red-tinted finger-nails. 'Can you fix it?' she asked. He nodded. 'I guess so.'

'You guess so. Don't you know?'

He nodded again. 'Yeh, I can fix it okay.'

A pause, and Sarah asked:

'Like soon? I mean I want to watch a programme. "This is Our Life".' She shrugged, half apologetically. 'I've been following it. It's my favourite. And it left off yesterday at such an exciting part. There's this young Doctor Brett whose wife is pregnant, and he's waiting for her in his office when this patient of his comes in. Blonde. You know, a real trouble-maker, you could tell right off. And she just grabs him. Just like *that*. And I mean, she's his *patient*, for God's sake. And there she is with her arms all wrapped around him when the door opens and this other doctor stands there. Mattison his name is. He's an older guy, nice, understanding, but you can see what he thinks . . .'

The mechanic grunted, not listening. Sarah went on,

'Well, you gotta admit, it looks pretty bad for Doctor Brett. I mean, he hadn't led her on or anything like that. She just went for him.' She shook her head. 'Yeh, it looks pretty bad for him.'

The man nodded, concentrating on his work.

'The programme begins in about seven or eight minutes,' Sarah said, and thought, Jesus, he's taking his time – the seconds ticking away, and he's acting like time didn't matter. She waited a moment longer, hovering aimlessly, then, turning to Laurie who was bouncing on the sofa cushions, said: 'Come on, honey. Come help me get the groceries from the car.'

As Laurie trotted out obediently behind her mother the TV mechanic shook his head with relief. These dames!

Back in the kitchen Sarah and Laurie put down the bags of groceries on the counter. Hurriedly, Sarah sorted out the things for the freezer, put them away, then made her way into the lounge again. The man looked up as she entered.

'That should just about do it,' he said. 'It only needed a slight adjustment.'

The picture now was steady, clear. Sarah moved forward and flicked the switch to the channel she wanted. 'I don't understand these things,' she said smiling. 'I just think you guys are so clever. It beats me.' She looked at her watch. Two minutes to go before the programme started. Shooing Laurie out of the way, she took her cheque-book from her purse and made out a cheque in payment of the bill the man presented to her. In seconds he was moving to the door.

'You shouldn't have any trouble,' he said. 'But if you do just give a call.'

'Yeh, sure, sure. Thanks a lot.' Sarah was hardly listening, most of her attention directed toward the flickering screen. Vaguely then she became aware that he had left the house and was walking away down the path. With a sigh of relief she kicked off her shoes and sank back into her chair facing the set. Seeing the sharp, perfect picture before her, she felt she could breathe again, relax. With the most exquisite sensation, she felt the tension just drain away.

As she tucked her feet up under her she became aware of Laurie at her elbow.

She gave a little sigh. 'Darling, why don't you go out and play for a while?' She didn't look at her daughter. 'Just while Mommy watches her programme ...' At the moment the afternoon movie was just ending. Next would come a bunch of commercials and then her show. She couldn't wait to see how Doctor Brett was going to get out of the spot he was in ... 'Go on, honey,' she prompted Laurie.

'You said we could have ice cream ...'

'Oh, I forgot!' My God, Sarah thought, these kids don't let you forget anything. 'Tell you what, sweetie – ' She turned a wide, empty smile in Laurie's general direction. 'Why don't you go into the kitchen and help your Mommy, yes? All the rest of the groceries – why don't you unpack them for Mommy and store them away? You know which ones go in the refrigerator, don't you?'

'The cold ones.'

'All the cold ones, yes. That's a smart little cookie.' (The commercials were starting now) She saw Laurie smiling, proud of herself. 'You think you can manage that?'

'Of course I can.'

'There's a good girl.' Sarah lit a cigarette and flicked out the match with a chewed nail. 'So – off you go, then, sweetie.'

Laurie started off, stopped. 'And can I have some ice cream, Mommy?'

Another commercial was just ending. 'What? Oh, it's in a block, darling. I can't get up just now. Can't you leave it till Mommy's programme is over?'

'But that'll be ages, and you promised.'

Sarah fought her rising temper, but even so the hardness crept into her voice, giving it that level, metallic edge that Laurie so hated to hear.

'I'll tell you what you do, sweetie,' Sarah said evenly. 'If you want it so badly you just go and get it yourself. You open the pack, cut off a slice, wrap the ice cream up again and put it back in the freezer. You got all that?'

'Yes, Mommy. Okay.' Laurie's little voice was docile. She started out again. At the door she turned and asked, 'And shall I get the syrup too?'

'Of course! If you want it!' Sarah snapped the words out. 'Now go on. Get out, for Christ's sake! Stop bugging me and leave me in peace!'

Her lower lip trembling slightly, Laurie nodded obediently. 'Yes, Mommy . . .' On tiptoe she hurried out of the room.

Left alone again, Sarah sighed with satisfaction and settled back once more. The programme was just about to start. She licked her lips and drew on her cigarette.

"This is Our Life" had been running for six years now, and Sarah had followed its involved plotting since its very beginning. Like many popular soap operas it covered the careers of a group of people, telling of their hopes, their fears, their lives and their deaths. Sarah felt that she knew each character. To her – as to many others – the people in the serial were real people, people who had no connection with the actors – the men and women – who portrayed them.

Now the blonde patient – oh, you could see what kind *she* was! – stood with her arms around Doctor Brett – just the way the last episode had ended, and there, standing shocked in the open doorway, the figure of the older man, Doctor Mattison. 'Oh, God,' Sarah said aloud, her hand to her mouth. 'Oh, my God . . . that poor man.'

In the kitchen Laurie was busy emptying the grocery bags. Very neatly, very carefully she unloaded the tins, bottles and packages. When she could reach the right shelf she stacked items neatly upon it; otherwise she placed them side by side on the counter before her.

The refrigerator door was heavy, but she managed it, and from the deep-freeze she took the block of peach ice cream and fumbled with the wrapping. It tore. Never mind, she thought, it wasn't a big tear. And there, at last, it was open, revealing a large pale pink block of luscious, tempting ice cream.

Moving the kitchen stool, she climbed upon it and took down a shallow glass dish. Then, taking a knife from the kitchen drawer she carefully sliced off a wedge of ice cream and slid it onto the dish. Afterwards, equally carefully, she rewrapped the ice cream block and replaced it in the deep-freeze. Mommy would be pleased with her, she was sure. All that was needed now was the raspberry syrup and the treat would be complete. Pursing her lips, she looked around. Where was the raspberry syrup kept?

On the screen in the lounge Doctor Mattison was looking gravely into the young, troubled, handsome face of Doctor Brett. The sexy blonde patient was nowhere in sight.

'You are aware of the seriousness of this . . . ?' asked Mattison.

'You don't understand,' the younger man said. 'It's not the way it looks at all . . .'

The next voice that Sarah heard was Laurie's, closer now as she called from the open doorway.

'Mommy, I can't find the raspberry syrup.'

Sarah flapped a hand, urging her to be silent. Laurie closed her mouth, waited. But no further sign was coming from her mother. Laurie tried again.

'Mommy, I can't find it. The raspberry syrup.' Sarah turned on her so suddenly that Laurie visibly jumped.

'Oh, for Christ's sake! What's wrong with you!? Can't you ever leave me in peace! What is it now?'

Laurie drew a deep breath. 'The s-syrup . . . the ras-raspberry syrup,' she stammered, trying to control her quivering lip.

'It's on the shelf above the refrigerator. Now leave me alone!' Sarah switched her attention back to Doctor Brett.

In the kitchen again Laurie climbed onto the stool, from there onto the counter, and then onto the refrigerator. Reaching up she opened the cupboard door. Right there, just as Mommy had said, was the bottle of raspberry syrup. Taking it carefully in her hand, she placed it on the counter and then climbed back down to the floor. It was done. She gave a little sigh of happiness and, taking up the bottle again, moved to take off the cap. It wouldn't budge.

Gripping it with all her strength, she tried again. No good. 'Golly gee!' Laurie breathed softly and then, loudly, she called:

'Mommy . . .'

After the call Laurie waited. And waited. No answer came from the lounge. The only sound she could hear was that of the music and the voices from the TV set. She called again.

'M . . . o . . . m . . . m . . . y . . . !'

Nothing.

The peach ice cream was beginning to melt. Laurie made another attempt to unscrew the bottle top. It was hopeless.

After hesitating for the briefest moment she made up her mind and, carrying the bottle, hurried into the lounge.

'Mommy –'

Sarah stubbed out her cigarette, her eyes never leaving the screen before her. She tried to close her ears to the persistent sound of Laurie's voice, to concentrate only on the fact that Brett's young, pretty, pregnant wife had just fallen down a flight of steps and now, unknown to her husband, was in danger of losing their unborn child.

'Mommy.'

The voice was there again. Sarah ignored it.

'Mommy.'

Sarah took a deep breath, her lips in a thin red line.

'Mommy, I can't get the top off.' Laurie stretched out her hand, holding up the bottle. Sarah ignored it, studiously. There was a long pause, then: 'The raspberry syrup . . .' Laurie ventured. Another pause, filled only by the voices from the screen. 'I can't open it, Mommy . . .'

Sarah whirled. First she slapped hard at the arm holding out the bottle, then she reached out and grabbed Laurie by the shoulders. She shook her. Hard. Once. Twice. She almost spat the words into the child's face.

'Then – go – with – out!'

With the words Sarah turned the child so that she faced the door. She gave her a push.

'Now get out! OUT! I swear that if you disturb me once more I'll . . .' Her words tailed off in impotent fury and Laurie, the bottle clutched in her trembling hands, scuttled back to the kitchen and the peach ice cream.

It was melting now. Its nice square shape was just dissolving away. Chewing on her lower lip she tried again to unscrew the cap. Still no good. With her tiny hands and weak grip she would never manage it.

Opening a drawer she surveyed the rows of kitchen tools. At last she chose a longish pointed object, lifted it out and firmly closed the drawer.

Holding the bottle tight in her left hand she rested it on the counter top. With her right hand she inserted the point of the tool underneath the lip of the bottle cap. And pushed. The next second the tool and the bottle had slipped from her grasp and fallen with a clatter into the sink. Laurie breathed a long drawn out sigh of frustration and stretched up, reaching as far as she could into the well. It was no good. Her reach was not long enough. She sighed again. Pulling the stool closer she climbed up, via the rungs, onto the counter top. Sitting there, perched up, it was an easy matter to retrieve the bottle and her improvised would-be opener. This time she held both objects much more firmly. Once more she carefully inserted the point, and again she pushed.

Nothing happened.

She pushed again. Harder still.

And suddenly there was movement. Sudden, terrifying movement as the tool slipped from the metal cap, skidded off the glass and gouged deep into the soft flesh of her wrist. Blood spurted, splattering her arm, splattering the countertop and the wall, splattering the melting pink peach ice cream. Laurie cried out in horror, pain and terror, 'Mommy! Mommy! Oh! *Mommy!*'

In the lounge Sarah tried to ignore her daughter's cries. Am I never to get any peace? she asked herself. Is it too much to be allowed, just for one hour a day, to relax? to watch one little TV programme without constant interruptions?

On the screen before her young Doctor Brett was still being confronted by the older man while, just yards away his wife lay unconscious, an anxious nurse leaning over her. For God's sake *do* something! Sarah pleaded silently with her. Do something! Don't just *stand* there! Then intruding on her concentration came Laurie's voice again, pleading, shattering the mood.

'Mommy!!! Please! HELP ME!'

Sarah's eyes remained focused on the picture as she yelled out:

'I'm warning you, Laurie! I'm warning you!'

The eyes of pretty young Mrs Brett pleaded with the nurse to help her. Her lips moved; it was obvious she was trying to say something. A slight sound came. Sarah leaned closer to the set. Mrs Brett's lips, pale, quivering, opened again, fluttering, nervous. The sound that came was Laurie's voice.

'MOMMY! YOU MUST HELP ME! PLEASE, MOMMY!'

Whatever young Mrs Brett had said, Sarah had missed it. And now the scene was changing again, jerking into the commercial break. Damn! Without a word she got up and walked from the room to the kitchen. There, without even glancing inside, she reached out for the door-knob, and with a swing that shook the house, slammed the door on Laurie's moans.

'Yell as much as you like!' Sarah shouted bitterly. 'I'm determined to watch this programme through to the end. So yell away. It won't do you a goddamn bit of good!'

She closed the lounge door as well, then, hurrying, back to her chair lit another cigarette and waited for the commercial break to pass.

Seeing the door slam on her, Laurie scrabbled to the edge of the counter. She was unaware of it, but the cries came from her throat like the blood from the artery in her wrist – in little short, regular bursts. She tried not to look at the gash, but it hurt so, and the blood just wouldn't stop coming from it.

'Mommy!'

She reached out a foot for a rung of the stool, but it was too far and the stool went over with a dull thud.

'Mommy . . . Mommy . . . Mommy . . . Mommy . . . Mommy . . . Oh, Mommy.' The only way to get down from the counter now was by holding onto the sink edge and lowering herself. Unless she jumped – but, no – that was too far, too high.

'Mommy, oh, Mommy.'

It was hard to hold on and support herself with both hands when her left arm hurt so bad. But she had to try it.

The crash that followed was the dish of ice cream smashing, shattering on the floor.

'Mommy! MOMMY!'

Mommy did hear, but Mommy took no notice, except to purse her lips even tighter and gaze unflinchingly ahead.

'Oh, please, Mommy ... Please ... I'll be good ... Please. Mommy ...'

It was impossible to hold on, what with the blood making it slippery, and the pain. Laurie fell, her feet slipping, skidding in the mess of ice cream and glass.

'Oh! MOMMY! PLEEEEEEEEEEEEEEZE!'

Sarah looked at her watch. Just four minutes to go. There had been no sound from the kitchen for some time now. Just as well, she thought. One had to be firm with children; it was the only way.

On the screen handsome Doctor Brett stood tall and strong, his wife held in his arms. He looked down at her, his eyes warm, crinkling at the corners while she looked up at him with a wan smile, brave, trusting. And then the screen flickered, the picture jumped and jumped again.

'*Christ!*'

Sarah leaned forward, moved a dial, flicked a switch. Nothing did any good. The scene before her was lost in a tumbling, cascading series of images falling one on the other. Faster, faster, and then the pictures were not pictures any more, but just flickering lights, dazzling and brilliant with blinding rapidity.

And then the lights stopped. The screen went blank. Nothing that Sarah did helped in the least. In the end she gave up trying. She straightened up, impotent in her rage. Just wait till she got hold of that klutz of a TV repairman. She'd have something to say to him!

Remembering Laurie, she crossed to the lounge doorway and shouted towards the kitchen.

'Laurie!'

There was no answer. The kid was probably sulking. Well, if she didn't quit it right away she'd get good reason to sulk. Kids these days – they thought they had to have everything their own way. Angrily Sarah strode across the hall and wrenched open the kitchen door.

'Laurie! Laur – '

At first, just for a moment, Sarah thought that the red was the raspberry syrup. But then she saw that it was not. The blood was everywhere, and in the midst of the mess lay the figure of her daughter, her blonde hair smeared with blood and ice cream and broken glass.

Sarah stood there, staring down. Then she opened her mouth and gave a loud, long terrified scream. Laurie's eyes, unmoving, their brightness glazed and dulled, stared at some point in space beyond Sarah's shoulder. Sarah screamed again.

But maybe there's a chance! she thought desperately. I must get a doctor, an ambulance, the hospital . . . Whirling, she ran for the telephone.

She was just about to pick up the receiver when the telephone rang. She snatched it to her ear.

'Hello . . . ?'

'Hello, Mrs Rooney . . . ?'

'Yes – ?' Get off the line! Get off the line! her mind was screaming. 'What is it?' she asked.

'This is the television repairman,' the voice said. 'I was wondering whether I might have left a bit of my gear behind at your house. I wonder if you'd mind looking by your TV set . . . It's a tool something like a screw-dri – '

Sarah's voice cut in, leaving him no further chance.

'You and your goddamn gear!' she said. 'You were supposed to have fixed my TV! You said I'd have no further trouble with it. No trouble, my ass! Can't a person depend on *anybody* these days?! Well, let me just inform you, Mr TV Repairman – Mr Efficiency, that because of you and your superior goddamn workmanship I have just missed a part of my favourite programme!'

GREEN FINGERS

S HE shouldn't have told me that I'd be one of the only three beneficiaries under her will. That's what caused it all. I had nothing against Aunt Ada. She was a harmless enough little woman, and really rather fond of me – she must have been, otherwise she wouldn't have made out her will, naming me, as well as Allan and Judith.

We were her only relatives. Allan was her second cousin, I believe, young and unmarried; while Judith and I are the children of her sister. Allan always struck me as being rather stupid, but mind you, my sister isn't likely to win any Brain of Britain contest either. I tolerate her, and have done for years, but we've never been on the same wave-length. Somehow our minds just don't go in the same direction. Both she and Allan have such mundane interests – as Aunt Ada did, herself – whereas I, on the other hand, am extremely sensitive and imaginative. One thing's for sure: neither Judith nor Allan could ever have conceived of anything like – that . . . Probably because they're basically *good* – if you can think of a more nauseating description of a person.

I had guessed for some time that I would be one of Aunt Ada's beneficiaries when she died. That was why I made all the regular visits to her cottage in Little Winborough. There, a couple of times a month I would listen to her chatter on about her flowers and her vegetables; her produce as she called it all.

'Come into the garden and see my produce,' she would say. There was always something so smug and irritating about the way she said 'my produce', but I put up with it – with a happy smile. I had to, I had to keep in with her.

Mind you, I wasn't alone in paying her visits. I know Allan called on her regularly, as did my sister Judith. Allan would roar up in his souped-up M.G., and my sister would go there by train. And there were even a few occasions that found us all visiting Aunt Ada at the same time – quite by chance. I don't know *their* motives for their visits to this rather sweet, boring old lady, but they certainly paid them often enough. Maybe their motives were the same as mine; maybe they also wanted to just keep in with her. I rather think, though, that Allan did it out of pure goodness (what a phrase!) and suffered Aunt Ada's interminable ramblings just to cheer her up. Judith, on the other hand, went, I think, because she genuinely *enjoyed* her company. Not having much up top herself, I think she actually found her sessions with the old girl *stimulating*. I do know that she was genuinely fond of her, anyway – but there, nothing surprises me about my stupid sister. I just thank God we don't have to share a house together. I left home long before our mother died, and now Judith and I rarely see anything of each other, which suits me fine.

This, of course, is all leading up to what happened on that particular Sunday. The last Sunday I visited Aunt Ada.

It was about time I called on her again, I thought, so I got into my small car (secondhand) and drove out to Little Winborough. Not an unpleasant drive, apart from a little boring engine trouble that held me up for half an hour *en route* – God, I *must* get a new car, I told myself. Anyway, the sun was shining, and a light breeze was blowing, and all told it was a good day for a visit.

I got no answer to my ring at the front door, and I guessed she'd be out on the garden. She always was whenever the weather allowed. Skirting the house, I went round to the back where her garden plot, surrounded by trees and a large, unused paddock, stretched down towards the river. Aunt Ada looked up as I walked along the garden path.

'Why, Tom-Tom – hello!'

Tom-Tom, her pet name for me since I was a child – and how I hated it. But I smiled at her, and she beamed all over her gentle, good-natured face, straightening as I approached, her gloved hand moving to brush back a wisp of grey hair that trailed over her bright blue eyes. 'What a lovely surprise!'

'Hello, Aunt Ada ...' I kissed her wrinkled cheek, warm and tanned from the sun.

'Somehow I knew you'd be here today,' she said. 'I just knew it. It's been one of those days. Dear Judith's only just this second left to get her train. What a shame you missed her.'

'Yes, what a shame,' I echoed, trying to make my voice sound genuinely sorry. Aunt Ada always referred to my sister as Dear Judith. God knows why.

'She'd have gone in the opposite direction, of course,' Aunt Ada went on, 'otherwise you'd have seen her on the road.' She looked at her little gold wrist watch, half hidden beneath the cuff of her gardening glove. 'And Allan'll be here any time,' she added.

'Allan?'

'Yes, he's due here any minute.' She gave me another bright smile. 'As I said, it's been one of those days.' She looked sadly back at the patch of newly-raked earth. 'I wanted to get this planted before Allan arrived. Still, it'll wait till tomorrow.' She clasped her hands before her, eagerly, like a child. 'When Allan gets here we'll all have some tea together. Won't that be nice?'

'Lovely,' I said, nodding my appreciation of the treat in store. Secretly I was beginning to regret my visit; I should have left it till *next* Sunday. But I kept my thoughts to myself, of course, and stood beside her and made the right comments about her garden. The vegetables and flowers grew in profusion. It really was a picture.

'It's really quite a picture, isn't it?' she said, as if reading my thoughts. I agreed with her and she beamed at me.

'Well, you either have green fingers or you don't. Some people do, some people don't. It's no special talent, and it's nothing you learn; it's just something you have or you don't have.' Her smile became arch. 'And I do. And I'm grateful.' She looked back at the garden, a blaze of greens, reds, yellows, blues, golds and pinks. 'I really do. And I'm glad and thankful. Look at it all. I don't mind saying that I'm really proud of my produce.'

'I'm afraid nothing would grow like that for me,' I said. I didn't know whether that was true or not – I'd never owned a plant of any kind – except once a friend had given me some potted flower – an aster, I believe – which lasted about two weeks. Well, who can remember to water those things? Anyway, it was the right thing to say to Aunt Ada; the quickest way to her heart was through her garden, and that was a fact.

And it was then, as she stood there beaming over her produce, that she told me about the will. I suppose it was the happiness of the day that made her confide in me. Dear Judith had just been to see her; I was standing there beside her, and second cousin Allan was on his way. She was feeling very much loved. And there again the sun was shining and her plants were growing. It all made a perfect day for her. And that's what made her tell – she must have been brimming over with happiness.

'I'm so lucky to have such thoughtful relatives,' she said. 'People who really care about me. I really am so lucky. And living out here, so secluded – no one nearer than the village, and that's half a mile away – one would expect to get dreadfully lonely. But you know, I *don't*. I always know that either you or Allan or dear Judith will be along to see me. I'm never alone for long.'

And that's when she mentioned the will. Sixty thousand pounds each, we'd get, she said. Sixty thousand. My God, it came as a surprise to me, I can tell you. I had thought maybe she had a few grand stashed away in the post office somewhere, but I'd never dreamed it ran into quite so much. Sixty thousand pounds each. Sixty thousand. Sixty thousand to be mine as soon as she died.

As soon as she died.

I looked at her standing in the sunlight with her gardening tools about her feet. She was a picture of health. For all her sixty-eight years she looked absolutely radiant, vital and bursting with life. She looked as if she could live for ever.

Almost as if reading my thoughts, she said:

'Mind you, Tom-Tom, I've got no intention of letting you have your money yet. Oh, no – none of you.' She gave a little chuckle. 'You're all going to have to be a bit patient. I intend to live for a very long time yet. There are so many things to do before I go.' She gazed down the garden and beyond it to the paddock. 'That paddock,' she said wistfully, 'I'd really like to get something done about that ... but it'll take *years* ... Still, I've got time. I'll get around to it someday.'

She would, too, I thought, taking in her rosy complexion and the smile that showed her strong white teeth. All that fresh air – all that plain, simple food – she looked as if she'd live to be a hundred.

'Allan is late,' she said, looking at her watch. 'Still – he'll be here soon.' She smiled at me and turned back to the little patch of finely sifted earth over which she had been stooping. 'I've grown dahlias here for the past few years,' she said, 'but this time I'm going to try something different. That's the secret, you know – variety in your produce.'

Her voice was full of happiness and satisfaction as she bent over the bare earth.

And it was then that I hit her.

I was still wearing my driving gloves, so I knew there'd be no fingerprints on the heavy stone I used against the back of her unsuspecting skull. I hit her three times, very hard. She gave a kind of choking moan and just crumpled, sagging to the ground. Then I ran back down the path and out of the gate. I had to get away before Allan arrived and saw me.

I did. I got almost a mile away before I stopped the car and sat nervously behind the wheel, my fingers drumming. I would have to go back, I realised. Now – this minute. I must. I wasn't even sure that she was dead.

There was no sign of Allan's car when I got back to the house. Thank God for his lateness. I hurried up the path at the back to where Aunt Ada lay sprawled on the earth, and came to a stop, looking down at her. And going by the position of her outstretched right arm, I realised that she had moved since I'd left her. *I hadn't killed her.* My God, that was a close thing! She was still alive! She could tell them everything.

And then, bending closer, I saw the deep markings she had gouged in the soft, fine soil, and saw what she'd been up to – what she had planned. And I laughed.

'Oh, you're a clever one, Auntie!' I said. 'It's a good job I came back – you'd have got me for sure.'

Quickly I picked up her trowel and scooped up quantities of earth which I then scattered over the letters of my name. Then, taking up the stone again I smashed it once more against her head. This time there was no mistake. I felt the bone of her skull cave in under the impact of the stone; I watched her eyes glaze over. This time when I left her there, she was quite, quite dead.

Outside the front gate I dodged behind a hedge just as Allan's car pulled to a halt before the house. I watched him get out and open the gate and vanish from my sight. Then, running, feeling quite exhilarated, I returned to my own car parked round the corner and drove away.

It had been so easy, I thought. Even if they did find out I was there they couldn't prove that I had killed Aunt Ada. I wouldn't even deny that I was there, I decided. Let them think I had nothing to hide. They had no proof that I had done the killing. After all, Judith had been there just minutes before me, and Allan had arrived just seconds afterwards. How could the police prove that either of them hadn't committed the crime . . . ?

As it turned out I was right. We all three of us had to undergo rigorous sessions of questioning, and all three of us stuck to our stories. Judith said she had left Aunt Ada well and happy and working on the garden; I said that I had had no answer to my ring at the doorbell and had left, thinking that she must be out; and Allan said that he had found her dead. I don't know whether Allan or Judith suspected me or each other but, like the police, whatever suspicions they had were useless without proof.

My God, but those police don't give up easily. Here it is, June, and they requested me (there's a polite way of putting it) to drive up to Aunt Ada's cottage and talk to them again. Well, they wouldn't get any further now than they had before – particularly after so much time has elapsed. I wasn't in the least worried. For one thing it was a sure bet that Allan and Judith would have to go through the same thing again. It was just a bore, that's all.

I drove my new sports car with the top down. I'm afraid most of Aunt Ada's money had gone now – but there, what's the good of money if you can't enjoy it. Mind you, the cottage was still to be sold, I reminded myself, so I'd get a bit more when that happened.

I really felt quite light-hearted as I drove. I sang at the top of my voice; I was so aware of the look of the countryside, the flowers, the trees, the sounds of the birds. Life was good.

There was no sign of Allan or Judith when I arrived at the cottage. But they'd be along later, I assumed. I did, though, see the uniforms of the police – but that was to be expected, of course, that's why I was there – at their request.

When I asked one of the officers if Judith and Allan would be arriving later they said they didn't think so . . . I thought that was rather odd . . .

Later I found myself standing in the living-room of Aunt Ada's cottage while they started again – asking me the same tired old questions all over again. I gave them the same tired old answers as before. Where was it all leading to? I'd thought that that was all just about done with. But there was something in the way they nodded at me; little looks passing between them which made it all not quite the same as before. It was almost as if they were listening to a well-played gramophone record where every sound is completely predictable. It made me nervous . . . They *knew* something, I thought; I could tell. And with the thought I could feel sweat break out under my arms and run down inside my new tailor-made shirt.

My anxiety grew when, minutes later, they took my arm and led me out into the garden. Skirting the hedge, I looked again at the patch of ground on which Aunt Ada's body had lain.

She lay there. Again. Her body was lying sprawled in exactly the same position in which I had left her; it was exactly right. But then all at once she got to her knees and I saw that it wasn't Aunt Ada at all, but just some policewoman got up in Aunt Ada's clothes. And she'd done it very well. Although her face was different, of course, everything else about her was just perfect – right down to her gardening gloves and the little packet she held in her hand. And seeing that, the packet of seeds, I started yelling again. I couldn't stop. The words just bubbled up out of me; I was screaming and babbling and I just couldn't stop.

I saw, so clearly now, the picture of myself filling in the deep gouges that Aunt Ada had made in the soft earth. I saw myself letting fall the fine soil, obliterating every single mark she had left on the surface. I had left no trace – no trace at all – I'd made sure of that all right. What I hadn't counted on was Aunt Ada's thoroughness. It was that that had given it all away – had given me away. I hadn't thought about the seeds.

Now, so beautifully, in letters two feet across, a glorious crop of cos lettuces spelt out her special name for me: TOM-TOM.